"The Pameroy mysteries never disappoint! I love how history gets mixed into the present. After reading this book, I really feel like I know Lillia and her Grauntie. Great read. Can't wait for the next!"

"What a fun mystery! I feel like I am right there with Lillia and Charlie during their adventures. Humorous, lighthearted and quite a page turner! I will definitely be recommending this one every chance I get!"

"Drawn into this book right from the beginning! My thirteen-year-old niece has read books in this series and loved them. So, it's been nice that we've both enjoyed and can chat about them! Great read not just for tweens."

"The Pameroy Mystery Series is such fun reading! I never figure out the ending until the last page. I can't wait to see what paranormal adventures will come next for Lillia and Grauntie!"

MYSTERY ISLAND

A PAMEROY MYSTERY IN MICHIGAN

BRENDA FELBER

Cover design-eBook Launch

Publisher-Laughing Deer Press

Publisher's Cataloging-in-Publication data

Names: Felber, Brenda, author.

Title: Mystery island: a Pameroy mystery / Brenda Felber.

Series: Pameroy mystery.

Description: Schofield, WI: Laughing Deer Press, 2019.

Identifiers: ISBN 978-1-948064-08-8 (pbk.) | 978-1-948064-09-5 (ebook)

Summary: The ghost of a little girl reaches out to Lillia to help reunite her with her parents. The discovery of mysterious shipwrecks help solve the mystery.

Subjects: LCSH Mackinac Island (Mich. : Island)--Fiction. | Straits of Mackinac (Mich)--Fiction. | Shipwrecks—Marine disasters--Wrecks--History—Juvenile Fiction. | Psychics--Juvenile fiction. | Friendship--Fiction. | Ghosts--Juvenile fiction. | Swindlers and swindling--Fiction. | Ghost stories. | Mystery fiction. | Supernatural--Fiction. | BISAC JUVENILE FICTION / Mysteries & Detective Stories | JUVENILE FICTION / Horror & Ghost Stories | JUVENILE FICTION / Paranormal, Occult & Supernatural | JUVENILE FICTION / Historical / United States / 20th Century

Classification: LCC PZ7.F33375 My 2019 | DDC [Fic]--dc23

ACKNOWLEDGEMENTS...

Couldn't do it alone...

A special thank you to Dionne Kelm for her constant support and clear-eyed, word-by-word read throughs. I'm so grateful to call this fellow author a friend and hope she keeps volunteering her efforts!

I'd like to take this chance to recognize and thank my love Mike for his unending patience with the days I spend researching, hours with my office door closed, and the times my mind is still working even as I sit next to him at dinner, on a hike, or in our comfy recliners.

I'm grateful for my cover designer's skill and talent... and his patience in working with me. Thank you to Dane at eBook Launch. Looking forward to the next forty-one!

CONTENTS

QUOTE TO PONDER...

"Now - bring me that horizon."

The last line from Pirates of the Caribbean.

Is this island real???

Yes it is...you can visit Mackinac Island! What you are about to read is a fictional story, but much of it involves places and things that are real.

For instance, cars are not allowed on Mackinac Island. You really do have to use horses or bicycles to get around.

Surrey Hill Square, Fort Mackinac, Arch Rock, Devil's Kitchen, the Grand Hotel, plus many other places are real. If you visit Mackinac Island you can see them.

The Pelletier family is fictional. But John Jacob Astor and Dr. Beaumont are real historical figures who lived on Mackinac Island.

There are hundreds of shipwrecks in the Great Lakes. If you don't scuba dive you can still find websites with terrific underwater photographs of them.

Please visit my website where I post photographs I used for inspiration in each of my stories. If you'd like to know more, I always welcome questions emailed to me at brenda@brendafelber.com

Happy reading,
Brenda

1

LILLIA

I couldn't wait to see Mystery Island up close. Would it be shrouded in fog with a spooky sinister aura surrounding it? Old wooden ships in the harbor, creaking as small waves rocked them. Strange, scowling men working on the docks, sliding their dark eyes in my direction. Eerie fog horns sounding in the distance.

The mystery stories I made up about the island kept my little brother Charlie entertained on our long drive. I like mysteries and they seem to like me. Travels with my great-aunt Nora usually involve mysterious happenings. One of Grauntie's Arizona friends had called the Michigan island we were headed to, Mystery Island. That stuck in my mind.

Grauntie Nora is always up for a trip. When Edgar and Dorothy Schmidt offered us their Mackinac Island cottage for a few days, I knew we'd be going there. This time Charlie wanted to go along too. He liked the idea of living on an island almost as much as I did.

There are no bridges to Mystery Island! With our suitcases in hand, we boarded an open-air passenger ferry in St. Ignace, Michigan. The island was a twenty-minute ride away. Charlie and I both raced for seats at the sides of the boat. The surface of the lake was calm and smooth as we pulled away from the pier.

Only a few minutes out, Grauntie Nora said, "Oh quick! Turn around. Look at that bridge. It's the one we drove over this morning."

It was ginormous! "Wow, I'm glad I didn't know how high above the water it is."

Over the loudspeaker the captain explained that the bridge was two hundred feet above the water and spanned five miles across the Straits of Mackinac. "It connects the upper peninsula of Michigan with the lower part of the state. On the other side of that bridge is Lake Michigan. We are on Lake Huron. The spelling of Mackinac Island often confuses tourists. It is pronounced Mack-i-naw. Now hang on and enjoy the ride!"

As we picked up speed, tiny droplets of water sprayed against my face. Feeling the lake air rush by felt wonderful after so many hours in the car. I closed my eyes and tipped my face to the sun. Four whole days on an island surrounded by a lake. Ahh...love it!

The captain's voice interrupted my thoughts as he began narrating our trip again. "The Great Lakes are an important liquid highway for the United States and Canada. They provide a vital passageway for cargo vessels. It is estimated that over six thousand shipwrecks lie at the bottom of the five great lakes...Michigan, Huron, Superior, Erie, and Ontario."

My younger brother Charlie leaned way out to peer over the sides of the ferry boat. Grauntie pulled him back. "Be careful Charlie, I don't think you'll see any shipwrecks under us, no matter how far you lean over."

The captain continued. "Thousands of ships have navigated through these Straits of Mackinac between Huron and Lake Michigan. The Straits have earned their reputation as a particularly treacherous area. Often shallows and rocky shoals put vessels at risk. Worst are the storms that push through here. The narrowing of this waterway as it passes between the Upper Peninsula of Michigan, and the main body of the state, magnifies the winds and waves created by those storms. Hundreds of vessels have gotten in trouble and sank. Many have never been found."

"Whoa," Charlie exclaimed. "That's cool."

"Cool?" I said. "That ships sink? People might have died. How is that cool?"

"Aw, come on Lillia, you know what I mean. It's spooky. Think about broken up ships and boats underneath us. Buried in deep murky watery graves." Charlie leaned over the back of my seat, waving his arms around my head. "You like spooky."

I swatted his hands away as I looked down into the water. He had a point. It was a spooky feeling thinking about boats lying in the water beneath us. We are traveling over a ship cemetery. How deep is this lake? What if our ferry sunk too? I looked around to assure myself life jackets were nearby.

As the island came into view, it was nothing like I'd imagined. Bright green wooded hills rose up above the lake's surface creating a brilliant contrast with the bright blue sky. A sprinkling of white buildings on the shore and up among the trees appeared as we got closer.

"That large white building is the Grand Hotel, famous worldwide for its spectacular location and world class amenities. Definitely worth your time to have ice cream at Sadie's or spend an afternoon on the wooden rockers lining the long front porch," the captain said.

The sun made the water around us sparkle and glisten as our ferry slowed, traveling parallel to the island. White mansions sat on a bluff, stately and elegant against the deep forest behind them. A small town nestled along the shoreline. I could see people moving along the sidewalks in the harbor area.

I wobbled as the ferry lined up against the pier, bouncing off the rubber bumper edging the dock. We had landed. As soon as we stepped off this boat, a sense of isolation hit me. We couldn't leave easily. Our only way off the island was by boat.

Sea gulls called overhead, ship horns sounded, and metal clanging against sail masts echoed across the busy scene.

"This place feels like it's frozen in time," Grauntie Nora said. "Just look at those buildings. They are over one hundred years old and still look great."

The buildings looked brand new to me. I was getting an island Disney vibe. Are they really that old?

Grauntie said, "No cars allowed here. Only horses and bikes. Just look at those big beasts pulling the cargo being unloaded. I feel like I'm traveling back in time." She swept her arms across the scene in front of us. "Amazing!"

I had to give her a little nudge. "Ah Grauntie, they want us to get off the ferry now."

Charlie waited on the busy dock next to our luggage. "So now where do we go?"

2

ARRIVING ON THE ISLAND

The large dock area in the harbor was busy and the St. Ignace ferry had to slow down to navigate into place alongside the pier. As passengers disembarked from the ferry, they became part of a scene that had been playing out since the late 1800s...tourists arriving to enjoy the beauty of Mackinac Island.

When one arrives on Mackinac for the first time, they invariably sense the specialness this place possesses. A sense of stepping back in time. The original period architecture is well maintained in the island's downtown commercial area. Summer cottages built by wealthy families edge the outskirts and stand proudly on bluffs above. Though calling them cottages is a bit of a misnomer... they are in truth, large mansions.

No automobiles wait near the dock to meet arriving

passengers. No taxis, limousines, or hotel buses line the street. No trucks are backed up to the wharf buildings waiting to load up cargo and materials from the mainland. Motorized vehicles are prohibited on the island.

Large draft horses, hitched to low sided wagons called drays, crowd the wharf area. The drays are being loaded with wooden crates and cardboard boxes from small vessels or from holds of large ferries. Produce crates filled with lettuce, melon, bananas, and tomatoes for the guests at the Grand Hotel are loaded on small wagons. Bales of hay to feed the horses leave the wharf on narrow flat wagons, heading uphill to the stables. Mail and small packages arriving for residents are placed into small, single horse carriages.

A shiny black carriage with the Grand Hotel logo displayed proudly on its side waited at the curb. The driver, dressed in livery from bygone times, stood ready to help hotel guests with their luggage. Smaller carriages, the equivalent of taxis, waited in line to offer a lift to arriving tourists. Two and four horse hitched teams pulled all manner of wagons, drays, and carriages on Main Street, plodding slowly past. No car fume odors, or engine noises marred the feeling of traveling back in time, when things moved at a slower pace.

In the middle of it all, stood a small, elderly man. His clothing, though well worn, was clean, pressed, and formal in appearance. He held his hat in one hand. His other hand held a sign high up in the air for arriving passengers to see. It read *Pameroy Party*.

"Okay, we've got our bags. Let's find a carriage taxi to take us to the Schmidt's house," Grauntie said as she made her way toward the street with Lillia and Charlie following along. "Stay right behind me you two."

"Why is our name on that sign?" Charlie asked, pointing toward the small man.

"Why look at that. Dorothy must have arranged a ride for us," Grauntie said.

The man stood near an elegant carriage. A pair of matching black horses with intricately braided manes were hitched to it.

"Hello. We're the Pameroys." Grauntie was almost giddy. "I've never been met by a driver before. I feel so special!"

"Well now, I'm quite sure you are special! Henry Thatcher at your service. I'm always glad to welcome arriving guests to Mackinac Island and the Pelletier House." He carefully put the sign down on the high front seat of the carriage and reached for our bags.

Grauntie, looking concerned, said, "Oh goodness, things must have gotten mixed up. I afraid we're guests of the Schmidt's not the Pelletier's."

Henry said, "My mistake. I misspoke. The mansions

here on Mackinac Island often keep the name of the original family who built the home. Dorothy and Edgar Schmidt own it now, but it will probably always be called the Pelletier House."

"Oh, I understand. Such history here. Will Dorothy and Edgar arrive tomorrow?"

"I wouldn't know about that ma'am. But I do know I was sent to pick you up." He extended a hand to Nora Pameroy to help her step up into the open-air carriage where two tufted leather bench seats faced each other. Freshly polished leather smells floated off the seats, completing the feeling of luxury.

Grauntie Nora seated herself. The spoked sets of wheels, small in front, large in back, rolled slightly as the horses shuffled in position. "Steady girls," Henry admonished.

He then turned to Charlie and Lillia. "Climb on in you young folk while I secure your luggage on the back rack."

Soon as Henry finished with the Pameroy's luggage, he hopped up into the high seat and reached for the reins draped in front of him. With a gentle snap of the reins and a soft *giddyup,* the pair of horses began to move. Henry carefully maneuvered the team into the flow of traffic.

3

LILLIA

We left the sounds and smells of the wharf behind as Henry maneuvered our carriage along the street. People pointed toward us, turning to watch as we rode by. It must be this carriage I thought. The light cream-colored leather seats and the graceful smooth curve of the wooden fenders was so different from other carriages. Our black horses, coats gleaming, harnesses polished, elegant arched necks and slender lean bodies so different from the big strong thick bodies of the work horses.

The gentle clop clop clop of hooves on pavement as we left the busy harbor area lulled me back to the way I felt with the sun on my face during the ferry ride over. No car engines or horns interrupted the quiet. Now, instead of Mystery Island, this is a feeling like I've time traveled. I feel like a princess on Magical Island!

Apparently, the horses knew their way to our house pretty well, because Henry was able to hold the reins with one hand while turning to talk with us. He pointed out interesting things along the way.

We made a turn to the right. The road ahead climbed a gentle slope and there stood a huge white building stretching against the hillside. "This is the Grand Hotel. You may have seen it from the ferry. It is famous world-wide," Henry said. "It was built in 1887. The front porch is six-hundred-sixty feet long. I can tell you all matter of facts about it, but might I suggest you experience it for yourselves? Your home for the next few days is only a short walk away so perhaps dinner here one evening?"

"The captain suggested Sadie's for ice cream," Charlie said.

Henry chuckled. "Sounds like a wise man."

I quickly added, "We always have ice cream for breakfast our first morning."

Now Henry laughed out loud. "Really now? I rather like that idea."

Our carriage crossed in front of the hotel where guests mingled on the porch and green grass lawns spilled down the slope.

After passing through the hotel grounds we continued upward. Soon we were on a street with the lake far down to our left and mansions rising up on our right.

"Look at the lighthouse out there." Grauntie Nora pointed toward a red and white tower on a peninsula of land jutting from a tiny island.

"Yes, ma'am that's the Round Island Lighthouse," Henry said. "It is no longer a functioning lighthouse but is being restored and protected as a local treasure. She took care of vessels going through this passage since shortly after the Grand Hotel was built. There's an automatic beacon now near the harbor's breakwater for signaling ships."

"How many lighthouses are in this area?" Grauntie asked.

"I believe a couple of dozen. Many of them are abandoned now though. Radar and technology have changed things so much ma'am." Henry called out *whoa* to the horses, pulling the reins in to stop us on the quiet street. His thoughtful posture held my attention. I watched him rest his hands in his lap.

"What is it Henry? Is something wrong?" Grauntie asked.

His profile as he looked out across the lake blurred, seeming to fade in and out. I think I was the only one who noticed it though because Charlie stirred restlessly next to me. I kicked him in the shins to make him knock it off.

"Nothing wrong. I was just considering that no

matter how careful captains are, how many ways they can be warned of trouble, the lake and Mother Nature still rule. She's taken many a ship down to a watery grave."

I thought I heard a soft sigh escape his lips, before he turned to smile at the three of us. "Sorry, got a bit off track there. But speaking of Mother Nature, I've heard there's a storm coming from the west. Appears it's moving faster than expected. Might consider adjusting your plans so you aren't caught outside somewhere when she hits." And with that he clicked his tongue, and the horses began moving again.

THE PELLETIER COTTAGE

Mackinac Island once served as an important hub for furs brought out of the interior regions surrounding the lakes. From beaver felted fur hats for men, to glamorous fur coats and stoles for women, demand was high. To meet the needs of trappers and buyers, local businesses sprang up providing lodging and supplies. The small town thrived.

From Mackinac Island, Louis Pelletier ran one of the more lucrative fur trading enterprises ever seen in the upper Midwest. French by birth, he followed in his family footsteps. Pelletier was the French occupational name for a fur trader. The family grew to love the island so much, that even after the fur industry died out, they built a summer cottage on the west bluff overlooking Lake Huron.

The Pelletier home, like many of its neighbors, was painted a clean crisp white. A large porch running along the front and around one side of the house, provided hours of relaxing pleasure for the family and their guests. Several smaller balconies are located on the second and third floors. The home has ten bedrooms and seven bathrooms. The elegant and detailed interior woodwork reflects true craftsmanship. Numerous fireplaces and stoves warmed the mansion over the years. Even after gas heat was added, the staff often lit a fire to fend off the evening chill.

The last family member to inhabit the home was Clarisse Pelletier. Early on she made the decision to stay there year-round. She lived in the house for almost her entire life, passing away in 1973. She became one of the very few people who spent the winter on the island. Clarisse chose to spend much of her fortune donating money to various island needs. When the breakwater required repair, she was the first to help fund the project. If a local child needed special medical attention, Clarisse helped the family with the expenses. She was loved by the local people. She was a private woman. She enjoyed gardening in the acreage surrounding the large home. On balmy days, she could be seen pedaling her bicycle around the perimeter of the island. Often in the late afternoon she would walk down the steep wooden staircase to enjoy a stroll along the beach. In the early evening, she could be seen high up on the third-floor deck watching the ships pass by in the twilight.

The elegant carriage with its three passengers traveled the bluff road and turned into the drive alongside the Pelletier cottage. Henry Thatcher assisted the Pameroys with unloading their luggage. He carried it to the side stoop and unlocked the door.

Light through the front windows cast beams deep into the living area as Henry stepped inside and turned on interior lights. He carried their luggage up the ornate staircase to the second floor, opening several windows to bring in fresh air. Something was astir here. He felt it. Very well then, let it begin.

When he returned to the first floor, Henry told Nora that he would be leaving them now. "Is there anything else you'll be needing ma'am?"

"Oh goodness no. This is just lovely. Thank you so much. I'm looking forward to taking your advice and walking back to the Grand Hotel for dinner," Grauntie Nora said.

"Good day then. Enjoy your stay." With a tip of his hat, Henry was gone.

Grauntie stepped out to the front porch and watched as Henry and his team of black horses rode away. She too took deep breaths of the fresh lake air. "Isn't this fabulous? Just look out there. Here we are on an island in this beautiful home. We are a lucky trio for sure and certain."

Charlie and Lillia ran back and forth along the length of the porch. Lillia twirled round and round. Charlie raced down the steps and did cartwheels in the overgrown front lawn grass.

Grauntie sank into one of the wicker chairs, her arms draped over the sides…totally relaxed. "I could live here," she said under her breath. Heavenly. And she closed her eyes to better feel the breeze off the lake.

She was startled when Charlie plopped down next to her with a bowl holding small glass objects. "Are these crooked marbles?" he asked.

"Why aren't these beautiful?" Grauntie Nora said. "They are called sea glass. Where'd you get that bowl?"

"From over there on the porch floor. What's sea glass?"

"These are from broken glass bottles that lake waves have pushed and tumbled for many years. The motion of rolling and softening the edges of jagged pieces of glass shapes them into these tiny little treasures. It takes a long time for the lake to break down glass pieces into sea glass. Not all beaches are capable of creating it. Good sea glass is hard to find. I wonder if Dorothy found all of these?"

"Do people just dump glass bottles in the water?" Charlie asked.

"No, I certainly hope not." Lillia joined them on the porch as Grauntie Nora continued. "But occasionally bottles might get washed out to sea during a flood."

"Or bottles from all those sunken ships?" Charlie said.

"Good point. Of course, there are also those bottles that are tossed out into the ocean or in big lakes with notes in them. Messages in a bottle. I heard of a woman in England who found one near her little cottage. It read *To my love Eloise. My desire is to return to you soon from this lonely place. Love you forever, George Peabody.* The bottle contained a photograph with some writing on the back. She hunted high and low, but never found Eloise. Years went by and she passed away but her granddaughter, using the internet, eventually found the children of George and Eloise Peabody."

Charlie looked bored, so Grauntie ended her story quickly. "A lovely love story about a note in a bottle. Oh my, the sun is sinking low and hitting me right in the eyes. Can you bring me my sunglasses please Lillia? They must be in my purse on the entry table."

"Sure." Lillia ran inside and soon called out. "Not in your purse."

"Oh darn, I must have left them in the carriage."

5

LILLIA

"Henry will find your sunglasses in the carriage and bring them back Grauntie," I said.

"I imagine he will," Grauntie said.

Charlie set the bowl holding the sea glass back on the porch. "Can I go and see that little house out back? It looks kind of cool."

"Sure, but be careful. Lillia, will you go with him? I'm going to get our things unpacked."

I really wanted to explore more inside the house first. But didn't want to end up helping Grauntie unpack. I said, "Come on Charlie."

Grauntie called out, "Oh and don't be long. Remember we're going to walk down to the Grand Hotel for dinner in about an hour."

Kicking my way through the tall grasses sent flitting

insects up. A dry dustiness rose up with them. The smell of old unused things, like dead left-over fall leaves that had escaped the rake. Apparently no one had been this way for many years.

Charlie, distracted by a small boat propped against the building, called out, "Hey, look at this. I wonder if we could use it for fishing." He rapped his knuckles against the bottom of the boat's hull and leaped back when a rabbit scurried out from under it.

I laughed. "I doubt it. Looks like it's really old. Probably leaks too. What's painted on the side there?" I pointed toward the weed covered edge of the boat.

Charlie tapped it once more. "Just making sure everyone inside there is gone," he said. He pushed aside a tall spreading weed with his foot and twisted his head to look at the image. "Looks like some sort of duck. Or a goose? Some kind of bird."

Charlie leaned against the building, his hands cupped on the small window to see inside. "Let's see if we can get in. It looks like an old garage."

"Can't be a garage. No cars allowed here," I reminded him.

"Maybe a stable then. Whatever you call it, there's lots of junk in there. Even an old carriage." He moved his head side to side. "Bikes, old tools."

The small door on the front was locked. We circled

behind the building. There was a fenced-in area in the rear. "This might have been where they kept horses," I told Charlie.

Wooden rough-hewn boards, resting on top of each other, formed the kind of crisscross fence we'd seen at Land Between the Lakes. The fence encircled a small area overgrown with weeds. This whole part of the grounds was no longer tended by any gardener. It couldn't be seen from the front of the house and tall evergreen trees hid it from the view of neighboring houses so they might have just let it grow wild.

"Over here," Charlie called out.

He had discovered a set of double doors. Each one was topped with small square windows. Large black hinges anchored them to the wall. The two doors were connected to each other with a latch like the gate to our neighbor's pool fence back home. Charlie lifted the latch out of its catch and the door began slowly swinging open on its own with a painful screech.

Dust filtered through the dim light coming in the building's small dirty windows. Things lay on the bare dirt floor and against the walls. Wooden boxes. Old rusty bicycles. Things I couldn't put names to.

"Look at this stuff," Charlie said. "Nobody's been here in a long time. These bikes are ancient."

I wandered toward the old carriage occupying the

middle of the room. Its body tilted, wooden hitching shafts resting on the dirt floor. Cobwebs attached themselves between the carriage and harnessing gear hanging on the wall nearby. This sure looked like the one we rode in today. The seats were cream colored too, but this leather was split open, worn and blackened with age. The carriage's wooden sides and fenders were dried out. Thin cracks ran along the wood's grain.

My mouth slowly dropped open as I watched cobwebs disentangle and float away. I let out a low breath as splits in the leather healed. Then gasped when, as if someone were wiping dust off a tabletop, a glossy waxed sheen appeared in a slow fluid motion over the curved wooden sections of the carriage. On the carriage floor lay Grauntie's sunglasses!

The translucent wavering figure of Henry Thatcher appeared, picked up her glasses, and handed them to me. He quickly put a finger to his lips to shush any words that might have come out of my mouth. Then he disappeared.

The dust settled back, dulling the wood's sheen. The cracks and cobwebs returned, eerily taking over the scene before me. Returning it to what Charlie saw as he walked up behind me. "Hey look, this sign, or crest, or whatever you call it, is the same as on the carriage we rode in today."

Knowing I'd had one of my imaginings and that I was seeing what others couldn't, I quickly decided to tuck the glasses into my short's waistband and pull my t-shirt over them before turning to answer Charlie. In a casual unconcerned sort of voice, I said, "It is? I can't say I noticed. What you got there?"

Charlie held a green bottle in each hand. "These bottles must be what Grauntie was talking about with the sea glass. Do you want to write a note to put in them?"

"Good idea Charlie. Let's take them back with us. Come on now, Grauntie Nora is probably looking for us," I said, glad he was so easily distracted.

6

DINNER AT THE GRAND HOTEL

Charlie raced ahead of Lillia. He pushed open the screen door calling out, "Grauntie we found green bottles. Can we use them to drop in the lake?"

Lillia slid in behind him, slipping the sunglasses out from under her t-shirt and laying them behind a lamp on the entry table next to Grauntie's purse.

"Charlie you can't just take them. They might be antiques," Grauntie Nora said.

"They were in some old boxes," he said.

"I don't care. We need to ask first." She reached for the two bottles. "These are quite lovely. Put them in the kitchen for now. If I get Dorothy's permission, I'll wash them out for you to use."

Charlie asked, "Why? The lake will clean them."

"Not on the inside Charlie. Plus, we'll have to find

something to seal them up with. Get ready for dinner now. There is a dress code so please wear pants, no shorts. And Charlie, I made sure your mom packed a nice button-down shirt for you."

Charlie groaned. "Seriously. Can't we just go to a McDonald's?"

"No chain restaurants on this island. Besides, I want to see the place. It won't kill you to put on something besides a t-shirt once."

As they came back downstairs, all cleaned up for the special dinner, Lillia stopped by the entry table. In a calm tone with just a hint of surprise in it, she said, "Why Grauntie Nora, aren't those your sunglasses behind this lamp?"

"What? I thought you looked there."

"You asked me to check in your purse."

"Well for goodness' sake, is my eyesight getting worse or my memory? As you kids say, whatever." Grauntie adjusted the glasses on her ears, peeked in the mirror to check her lipstick, and strode out the door.

Lights were turning on inside cottages along the bluff. People sat on their porches waving and called out good evening to the threesome. Dogs greeted them before returning to their own yards. Deep shadows covered the forest behind the homes.

As they approached the hotel, hints of music floated

across the air. Colorful flowering plants perfumed their path. Couples strolled arm in arm. Children raced across the generously sized lawns, chasing the first fireflies to appear.

"Grab a rocker here on the porch," Grauntie Nora said. "I'll step inside and let the maître de know we'd like a table." She disappeared through the big glass doors of the hotel.

Lillia and Charlie found three chairs on the long porch. "I'm going to walk this out. Check if it is as long as Henry said. Six hundred feet, right?"

"I think he said six hundred and sixty," Lillia said. "Take a really long stride. That's about three feet. I mean like really… really long. And if you divide three into six hundred and sixty…"

"Hey, I could have done that if you gave me a minute." Charlie shot Lillia an annoyed look. "Besides I want to take tiny footsteps." He hurried to one end and began his measuring.

Transition from day to evening was happening. The enormous lobby chandeliers were lit. Hotel guests gathered in the numerous sofas and chairs. The dining room began filling with people. In front of the hotel, the sunset threw soft oranges and purples across the water as she rode the last edges of the horizon.

Grauntie returned. "That was quick. Where's

Charlie?"

"Measuring the porch," Lillia said as she waved to her brother to hurry.

"But I didn't get done," Charlie grumbled. "I'm only to eighty-nine steps."

"I think we can confirm the length with our waiter," Grauntie said with a chuckle. "I'm hungry!"

After being seated and ordering dinner entrees, Grauntie Nora took a sip of her wine. "So now you two, if Dorothy agrees you can use those green bottles, what do you think you'll write on a note to put in them?"

Lillia and Charlie seemed stumped. Nora decided to give them a few minutes to think. She looked out the window, past the porch. The Straits of Mackinac stretched out from under the sliver of sunset left. Stars hung in the night sky. So quiet. So peaceful. Such a special place, she thought. *I can see why tourists enjoy this island.*

"I'll write a note about me," Charlie finally said. "I'll write the date and place. That would be about it. Maybe I'll put my phone number or address. If someone finds it, they could let me know. Yep, I'll do that. I'll ask them to contact me and let me know where they found it. Maybe it'll be far away."

The waiter reappeared with their salads.

Charlie was still absorbed in his note ideas. "I

wonder, could it make it out to the ocean?"

"Charlie, we're on a lake," Lillia said. "It could maybe go under that big bridge to the next lake, but that's about it."

The waiter cleared his throat. "Excuse me, but may I add to your conversation?"

"Please do," Nora said.

"Technically, a bottle put in Lake Huron from the shoreline just steps away, could make it out to the Atlantic Ocean. It would be difficult but from Lake Michigan, the Illinois River would get it to the Mississippi, and that would take it down to the Gulf of Mexico, which of course would allow it to float on out to the ocean. From there it could travel round the world."

"Whoa man! Cool!" Charlie turned to Lillia. "Guess you don't know everything?"

Lillia grinned. "Guess I don't."

"And if I may, I'd like to add that the St. Lawrence Seaway also provides ships navigable waters from these lakes out to the Atlantic via the St. Lawrence Seaway."

"What's navigable mean," Charlie asked the waiter.

"It means ships can travel it. They can navigate their way through. The Great Lakes see barges and container ships from all around the world."

Charlie couldn't believe it. "So, my note could make it to anywhere in the world?"

I never did get to say what I would put in a bottle. Guess it was no big deal to me. But I was amazed to learn how all these waters are interconnected. How Charlie's bottle could end up in Chicago or Mexico or Japan!

Dinner finished, we were walking down the porch steps when the waiter came running after us waving Grauntie's sunglasses in the air. "You left these on the table."

He was startled when we all started laughing!

"Thank you. I think I need one of those string things that hang glasses around my neck. This is the second time today I misplaced them."

I couldn't help but think this time the man who returned them was real! Not one of my imaginings.

On the second floor Charlie and I were set up to

share a room with twin beds. I knew he still had a lingering fear of the dark, especially in strange places. I figured Grauntie put us together so Charlie won't be alone because there were lots of bedrooms.

This bedroom felt like it hadn't changed since the house was first built. I knew the Schmidt's used the home over the summers, but so many things seemed original, like these old brass headboards. The quilts were a little musty smelling and had uneven hand stitching like the ones I saw in the Historical Society display in Wisconsin. The curtains thin and faded from the sun.

A door led to a porch holding white wicker furniture with green and white striped cushions. From this second story porch I watched the channel marker's light blinking. In the distance, lights on some slow-moving vessels flashed on and off. Far away I saw a small glob of lights. Wonder if that's a little town on the mainland?

Feeling restless, I thought of Henry Thatcher. He let me know something was up when he handed me the sunglasses. Henry must be my spirit guide. And where there's a spirit guide, there's a local mystery for me to solve! I wondered what it might be. Why even that beautiful team of horses probably wasn't real! What a perfect setting for my abilities to piece together energies from the past. My imaginings. This whole place was like in the past!

I shivered. It was getting cold out here, so I went back inside to get the quilt from my bed to wrap around my shoulders. Charlie was fast asleep. I tiptoed around and was picking the quilt up when I heard the first sound, a faint tap. I stopped to listen.

Probably nothing...old houses have creaks and groans.

Tap tap.

Footsteps? They seemed to be coming from above me. I knew there were rooms up there. Tap tap tap. Charlie and I had explored the staircase to the third floor.

Tap tap tap tap.

There was a carved wooden door at the top of stairs, and it was locked.

My heart jumped out of chest when a loud scraping sound came from the balcony. I hugged the quilt against me like a shield and peered out the door.

Whew it was Grauntie! She was dragging one of the chairs closer to the balcony.

"Grauntie," I whispered. She didn't hear me. I tiptoed out and tapped her on the shoulder.

She jumped and spun in one move. "Oh, you scared me! How did you get out here?"

I pointed to the door from my bedroom. Grauntie pointed to a second door cleverly hidden by angled walls. Each of our bedrooms had access to this little porch.

Clever design. I wondered if there were secret passages like at I'd seen at the Biltmore Estate in North Carolina.

"The night sky is so clear, and the stars go on forever. It's unearthly peaceful here now. I can see why people come here to get away. We're isolated, but in a comforting way."

"This house feels extra old doesn't it?" I asked.

Grauntie chuckled. "It is old sweetie. But I know what you mean. Kind of in a spooky sense, like the whole island. Time has stood still here."

"Grauntie, were you tapping on the wall just before you came out? Or maybe you bumped against some furniture and it made a noise?"

"No, just walked out here." She stuck out her feet so I could confirm that she was in her knit slippers. "And I cleared all the wall between my bedroom and this balcony without bumping into it once."

"Ha ha. I thought I heard noises though. A tapping sound. It came from above our room."

"Oh gosh! I hope raccoons didn't get in. Or chipmunks either. Let's go up and check it out," Grauntie said.

"But the one door there is locked."

Grauntie thought a moment. "I'll bang on the door so we can hear if anything scurries off."

When we knocked on the carved door, no sounds

came from the space behind it. "Hmm, tell you what. Liam's going to be here later tomorrow. I'll mention it to him. If those animals get in, they can do so much damage. Let's both try to get to sleep now. Night Lillia."

"Night Grauntie."

I climbed into bed and closed my eyes.

Tap.

My eyes popped open. I didn't breathe.

Tap. Tap.

That was not an animal.

Tap. Tap tap. Tap tap tap.

8

FIRST MORNING ICE CREAM

"Hear any more strange sounds last night Lillia?" Grauntie asked as Lillia and Charlie came racing downstairs. She knew they were up early because of the ice cream for breakfast tradition. It had started the very first time she took Lillia on one of these trips. She decided long ago that she was blessed to be able to travel with her grandniece and grandnephew across the United States.

Charlie came to a sudden stop on the third step from the bottom. "Strange sounds? What strange sounds?"

Lillia swerved to avoid him. She jumped off the last two steps and looked back up at her brother. "Footsteps and stuff like that. In the third-floor attic."

"Grauntie, tell her not to tease me," Charlie whined.

"For goodness' sake, I don't know what she heard. Old houses make noises."

Charlie shot a glare towards his sister. "That door was locked. We tried it. There's nothing up there."

Lillia shrugged. "Chill Charlie okay? Might be animals in the attic. Squirrels, raccoons."

Charlie seemed relieved by that. He pulled his baseball cap tight down on his head as he walked past Lillia.

"Okay, off we go to Sadie's for our ice cream," Grauntie said.

Morning dew still clung to the lawn grasses as the three started the walk to Sadie's. The lake glistened in the angling rays of morning sunshine. Butterflies flitted about on the flower beds lining the lawns. Birds swooped overhead, flying from tree to tree.

Grauntie enjoyed the clean freshness of the air. After ice cream she had plans to do a horse and buggy tour. This would be the perfect day for it. "I hope Dorothy's grandson Liam gets here today. It'll be so nice to see him again. He seemed like such a nice young man when we met him in Arizona. Oh, and Lillia, I'll try to get a key to that third-floor door from him. Plus I'll talk to Dorothy too and see if it's okay that you kids go up there."

"Don't forget to ask her about those green bottles," Charlie said. He saw the sign for Sadie's and ran ahead.

By the time Grauntie and Lillia walked in Charlie had already picked out his flavor. "Waffle cone with Deer Traxx. It's got peanut butter cups and chocolate fudge!"

"Good morning. This young fellow assures me he has your permission to order ice cream for breakfast. Is that true?" The man behind the counter held a scooper, ready to make Charlie's cone.

"Yes, it is," Nora said. "But don't spread that around. I have a reputation to maintain as a good Grauntie!"

"What, may I ask, is a grauntie?"

"It's a mashup of great-aunt and grandaunt. My brother, God rest his soul, was their grandfather," Grauntie Nora said. "Now let's see, you've got Charlie's order…" She took a minute to scan across the flavors posted on the sign. "I think I'll try black cherry. Lillia, what about you?"

"Are you staying here at the hotel?" the man asked as he scooped black cherry in a bowl.

"No, we are guests of the Schmidt's. They have one of the homes on the bluff."

"Don't recognize that name I'm afraid."

"It's the Pelletier house Grauntie. Remember what Henry told us?" Charlie said before taking another big lick of his ice cream.

Without looking up from scooping orange cream swirl for Lillia, the man said, "I always heard that place is haunted."

"Haunted?" Charlie's voice jumped to a high tone in the empty ice cream parlor.

The man sensed Charlie's fright. He looked up at Grauntie and winked before saying, "Oh. Wait. No. Sorry. That was the house next door to that it."

Charlie didn't fall for it. "You guys said you heard something last night. Are we staying in a haunted house?"

"Lillia did hear something last night Charlie," Grauntie said. "I'm assuming something got in the attic. Pretty common occurrence in a house closed up for the winter. I'm going to have Liam make sure to check it out as soon as he gets here."

Charlie looked skeptical. Should he believe it was only animals? He straightened up his shoulders. He'd face his fears head on. It's just a house. A very old house. A house where no one lives for months and months of cold, snowy, bitter, icy winters. A perfect house for a ghost. He shook his head to stop the avalanche of spooky thoughts. Knock it off Charles Pameroy. You're eight years old!

With a wave goodbye to the man who'd served them, Grauntie said, "Okay kiddos, we'll finish our ice creams outside. I've got a carriage ride tour set up for us!"

9

LILLIA

A three-horse team was hitched up to the touring carriage. Black harness straps crossed their big rounded rumps. Large collars, with silver knobs sticking up, rose above their thick strong necks. Blinders on the bridle of each horse shielded their eyes from distractions, keeping them focused forward.

"What are those things draped across their backs? They look like a fringe or something," I asked the guide standing nearby.

"Those are called fly nets or fly chasers. They help prevent flies from bothering the horses," she said. "Are you joining us on the tour today?"

"Yes, we are," Grauntie piped up as she came over with our tickets. "This is our first time on the island. I thought this would be a perfect way to get acquainted with it."

The tour guide reached for the tickets. "It is the best way."

I hurried to get on. I wanted an outside edge seat to get good views without having to look past someone's nose or through their hair.

The guide helped me up the step and into the carriage. "You've got such pretty hair. It's the same beautiful chestnut color of our team. You even have braids like them. And their eyes are brown like yours." I wasn't sure about being compared to the three large horses hitched up to our ride!

Soon the carriage driver called a *gettyup* to the team, and we were on our way.

The tour guide began by explaining that these types of guided tours had been operating on the island for over one hundred and fifty years. "But Mackinac Island, notice I pronounce it Mack-i-naw, wasn't always just a tourist spot. Archaeologists excavated prehistoric fishing camps on the island dating back to AD 900, finding fishhooks, pottery, and other artifacts. This area was rich with fish. During the mid 1800s fishing was a very lucrative industry here. Then the fur trade, which had always found a home in this part of America, blossomed when fashion dictates out of Europe, New York, and Chicago greatly increased the demand for it."

We turned on to the bluff road where our house was. The guide briefly described each house as the driver drove past them. "From famous industrialists to wealthy artists, these so-called cottages have graced our island for many decades."

As we approached the Pelletier house she said, "This cottage was built by the Pelletier family from France who amassed a fortune during the heydays of the fur trade industry. This cottage, or should I say mansion, is one of the larger ones on the island. The original stables and carriage house still stand on the grounds. Please note the architectural design includes porches and balconies on every floor, giving occupants numerous places to enjoy expansive views of the lake."

I was looking up at our house, along with all the others on the tour, when one of passengers started waving. There was someone standing on the small third-floor balcony waving back!

I leaned out to see better. It looked like a woman. I nudged Grauntie. "Quick, look up there. There's someone in our house." Well you'd think I'd said I was a princess or something!

"You live there?"

"Lucky you!"

"What's it like?"

"Are there really ten bedrooms? How many baths?"

Grauntie looked at all the expectant faces and smiled awkwardly. "It's a lovely home. We are just guests of the gracious owners."

By the time Grauntie got a chance to look up the woman was gone. She leaned toward me and whispered, "I don't see anyone. You must have just seen a shadow. Dorothy didn't tell me about anyone staying with us."

I wasn't convinced it was just a shadow. After all, the first person to wave was one of the passengers. Someone else did see the figure. And those sounds last night. I'm sure they were footsteps from someone moving around on the floor above my bedroom. The third floor.

Grauntie patted my knee and tipped her head towards Charlie to remind me he might be listening. "No worries Lillia. I'll ask Dorothy what's going on. We'll talk later." She made a point of speaking louder when she said, "Now shh, listen to the tour guide."

10

CARRIAGE TOUR

Charlie overheard Grauntie tell his sister to be quiet. He felt a small guilty nudge of pleasure. Usually those words were directed to him. This part of who built what and who lived where wasn't very interesting to him. It was the lake that captured his attention.

He remembered what he'd been told about the shipwrecks out there. As the tour continued along the bluff road, he got a view of the Mackinac Bridge. A large barge carrying shipping containers moved slowly under it while a steady line of car and truck traffic flowed over the bridge. He wondered what was on that barge. Where was it headed? To travel the seas intrigued him. He was mesmerized, lost in thought, only to be interrupted by the tour guide saying, "I see you're very interested in the scene across the lake young man. Do you have any questions for me?"

Charlie answered, "I'd like to hear about the ships and what they do. What happens to all the freight moving around on the Great Lakes in the winter? Does it just stop? Does the lake freeze over? Are there really lots of shipwrecks on the bottom of the lake?"

The others in the tour group chuckled as the questions flowed out of Charlie. He noticed and with a reddened face stopped asking. He'd made a fool of himself.

Except the tour guide didn't think so because she said, "Those are great questions. I appreciate being able to talk about them."

Charlie was relieved and settled back to hear her answers.

"Let me start with the questions about winter. Occasionally the lake does freeze over hard enough to give this island an ice bridge to the mainland. People are allowed to snowmobile to the island when that happens. There are ships called ice-cutters that are specially made to break up the ice and keep the shipping lanes open. Many shipwrecks have been found and mapped. Some ship's wreckage is never found." Everyone listened intently as she went on to share information about cargo moving on the Great Lakes.

The carriage horses turned, entering a cool shady forest. Sheltering trees edged closer to their path. The first stop was a small cemetery surrounded by a white picket fence. A curved wooden archway entrance read *US Post Cemetery Fort Mackinac.* The tour guide stepped down from the carriage to speak to the group. The driver removed his hat and joined her. The tour group stopped chatting to listen.

"This is Post Cemetery, a designated National Historic Landmark. I imagine you noticed the United States flag on many of the headstones. Those graves date back to the War of 1812. We have both American and British soldiers buried here. Often times early markers were simple wooden crosses that have long ago disappeared. Less than half of the over one hundred buried bodies have their gravesites marked. I'd like you all to take note of the flag flying at half-mast. This is an honor bestowed on only four National Cemeteries. We here on Mackinac are honored to have our Post Cemetery recognized as one of them."

"It must be sad to be buried so far away from your home country like this," someone said.

Charlie, with his newfound confidence in speaking up, told of his visit to Massachusetts. "There were British soldiers buried in Concord too. They were killed in the Revolutionary War."

"Really? That's very interesting. Thank you for sharing." The guide gave him a thumbs up as she and the driver climbed back into the carriage.

A couple sitting next to Charlie remarked on his knowledge about American history.

"I love your accents," Grauntie said, turning to speak to them. "French?"

"French-Canadian," the woman said. "We're exploring early French and Canadian influence in America. We were interested in the fur trader Pelletier. Earlier we overheard that you were staying at the Pelletier home."

"We are. This is my grandnephew Charlie and my grandniece Lillia. We don't know much about the history of the house, but yes it was built by the Pelletier family. Are you enjoying your trip so far?"

"Oh yes. We are interested in the waters here as is Charlie. Our journey begins here because this is where Louis Joliet and Father Jacques Marquette began their expedition to find the Great River or Messipi as the Native Americans called it."

Charlie joined in. "What river is that?"

"The Mississippi. They hoped it would lead them to the Gulf of Mexico, providing a waterway from the northern reaches of this country."

"The waiter last night told us there is a way from here to the Gulf. The great water highway. Lake Michigan to the Illinois River to the Mississippi and then all the way down to the Gulf of Mexico," Charlie proudly recited.

"And he was right about that. Father Marquette and Joliet missed the Illinois River. In Wisconsin they portaged from the Fox River to the Wisconsin River, which took them to the Mississippi. Remember, they didn't have maps then. It was in the mid 1600s. They made it most of the way to the Gulf but ended up turning around to head back because of the heavy Spanish presence in the southern parts of America."

"Why did that matter?" Charlie asked.

"Joliet was born in Quebec, like us. It was founded by French settlers. Marquette was from France. But America was being explored and claimed by different countries. The small expedition of men in their canoes didn't want to confront the Spaniards. Too few on the expedition and too many of the Spanish."

Grauntie and the couple chatted about the value of travel as the tour continued through the forests and to a paved parking area where they would be stopping to water the horses.

They were back at the edge of the lake again. This time high above the shoreline. Most of the group wandered off on a short trail to see a large rock that had been hollowed out by weather...Arch Rock.

"Just look how little those people look," Grauntie

said, pointing down to several bikers on the shoreline road below.

The Canadian couple remarked, "We did an eight-mile bike ride that circled the island yesterday."

"Charlie, Lillia, did you hear that? I'm up for doing a long bike ride tomorrow!

"Eight miles seems kind of far," I said. "Do you think you'll be okay with that Grauntie?"

"I hope so," she said. "Looks like it's a pretty flat road. It's the hills that I can't handle. If there are any, I'll just walk 'em."

The horses finished getting their fill of water and our tour group loaded up again. We headed back inland away from the island's eastern edge, circling behind Fort Mackinac.

The guide explained, "Our last stop is Surrey Hill Square. Please tour the two carriage museums and be sure to take time to enjoy the grounds. Additionally, you can walk over to see our horses enjoy down time in the pastures. After you've visited you can take the next carriage to town or enjoy a short stroll down the hill. Either way, we enjoyed having you along."

After a round of applause, we all left the carriage. Grauntie wanted to walk through the museums first. "And I'm going slowly…reading every sign," she warned Lillia and Charlie. "How about you come with me in one of them and I'll do the second one myself?"

I had to laugh at Charlie's groan because I knew how he felt. But it sounded like a good compromise so in we went.

I was overwhelmed by all the styles of buggies that had been refurbished for display. A large black-and-white photograph hung above a particularly fancy carriage. The description read that this was the Pelletier family in front of Fort Mackinac in1887. In the carriage sat a young girl alongside an elegant couple smiling in the summer sunshine. So that's the family!

The man holding the horse reins while the photographer took the picture looked like Henry Thatcher. This put a lot of things in place for me. A small smile tickled the corners of my mouth. My spirit guide had been a driver for the family whose house we are staying at.

Grauntie called to me. "Come along Lillia, I'm ready to check out the other museum."

I gave a tiny wave of my fingers toward the photograph. Henry waved back! And he smiled right at me!

Did he want me to know something? To help with something?

"Grauntie, you said we only had to go in one of these stable museums," Charlie complained.

"You're right. After this one, you two can run off and see whatever you want. I know you're full up on facts about Mackinac, but I'm not. I'll grab a coffee when I'm done and wait for you right outside here."

Charlie and I took off running. We soon discovered a pasture where the big horses were free of harnesses and bridles. They looked like kids let out at recess. Pawing the ground. Prancing in odd little dances. Dropping to their knees to roll in the dust. They were having fun! We stood side by side on the fence rail and watched these big gentle giants lay on their backs and roll side to side, before leaping up to shiver and shake. Suddenly dipping their heads down and then flinging them back up.

Grauntie came to find us. "Well this is a twist. Usually you two are ready to go before me."

On the way out of Surrey Hill Square, Charlie noticed what was called an Indian Weather Rock hanging from a tripod of rough-hewn logs. Carved in a board above the large suspended stone were the words…

Genuine Old Indian Weather Rock

If rock is wet-it's raining.

If rock is white-it's snowing.

If rock is moving back and forth- it's windy.

If rock is hard to see-it's foggy.

If rock is casting a shadow-it's sunny.

If rock is cold-it's cold out.

If rock is warm-it's warm out.

Old Indian never wrong.

"Are they making fun of the Indians?" Charlie asked. "This seems kind of mean."

"Nonsense. If anything, it might be put here to make us pause to consider the simplicity of life long ago. Now we have so much information in these little things in our pockets. What's the weather? People whip out their phones and have the forecast for the next week, hour by hour."

"But isn't that progress?" I asked.

"Yes, but wouldn't those Indians be puzzled by how much time we spend with our noses in those handy dandy little things, reading this, looking for that, sending a text instead of talking to those around you? Or just being present in the moment? Like the rock idea…"

"Like KISS?"

"That's right Lillia. Keep It Simple Stupid," Grauntie

said. "Simple is what that weather rock represents. Sometimes our modern world complicates things. The Indians would not be offended by that weather rock display Charlie. They'd more likely find humor in our dependence on technology to tell us it's raining!"

12

LIAM ARRIVES

Back in the village, Liam Schmidt stepped off the ferry boat from St. Ignace. It felt good to be back. He waved to the driver of a team of work horses waiting to load up his dray with cargo from the ferry's hold. "How's it going Sam?"

The driver, waiting in a line of wagons, said, "Hey there Liam. Haven't seen you around much this summer."

Liam laughed. "We all have to grow up sometime man. How's business?"

"Better than ever. Busy season once again. Excuse me...duty calls." He was being signaled to get his horses in line to pick up produce. "The hotel guests will want their melons for the morning. *Giddyup* there girls," he said as he touched his team's rumps with the reins.

Liam didn't bring a suitcase as he planned on leaving

the island later today. Word was that a storm forecasted to arrive in a couple of days was moving much faster than expected. The dive boat operation moved up their next excursion hoping to get out to the shipwreck ahead of the storm.

Liam was excited to dive again tomorrow. He'd gotten some great underwater photos of a wreck yesterday. Plus, he noticed something else, nearby and through the murky water, that looked interesting. He hoped to get time to check it out when they went back down.

He took a deep breath of the clean, cool, balmy air. The time he spent here was the highlight of his summers. Time with Grandpa and Grandma Schmidt at their summer home, running along the beaches, horseback riding, taking his bike around the island, and yes, all that fudge to eat.

It was too bad that Grandma's hip was acting up again, but he hoped to see them within the next couple of days.

When Grandma asked him to interrupt his dive trip to check in on the Pameroys, he was happy to. He looked forward to seeing them again. Meeting Lillia on the packing trip to Reavis Range in Arizona had been fortuitous. Her solving of the whole thing about the Superstition Curse hitting the Bender family was amazing for such a young girl. She inspired his mystery writing with her abilities.

He'd learned from Grandma that Nora had planned a carriage tour for this morning. If he timed it right, he'd probably find them walking down the hill from Surrey Hill Square.

He sat on one of the many benches in Marquette Park to keep an eye out for the Pameroys. It was a beautiful day. Blankets created a patchwork of color across the sun warmed lawns as families gathered to picnic. His eyes closed instinctively as his face turned up to accept the sunshine. A tap on his shoulder made him jump.

"Looking for us?" Lillia giggled and pointed toward her grandaunt Nora and a boy who must be her brother Charlie.

"How'd you sneak up behind me like that?"

"I saw you here on the bench. Easy to sneak up on someone with his eyes closed!"

"I guess I was sort of dozing. Did you guys have fun on the carriage tour?"

"We sure did," Lillia said. "And we just got done at the stables. Those are some huge horses! I'm so glad you're here. What a cool place your grandparents have."

"And I'm glad to see you again. We can talk a little mystery!"

"Speaking of mystery, Charlie and I tried to get in the

attic, but it was locked. Do you know if there's a key for it?" Lillia said.

Grauntie Nora reached the two and said, "Excuse her, Lillia is always the curious one!"

Holding his palms up in surrender Liam said, "No I don't know where a key is, sorry. And…ah…I might be the reason the attic is locked. There were a few times when I, as a much younger and immature person you understand, might have given my grandparents reasons to reconsider giving me the run of the house."

Nora nodded sagely. "So, are you saying it's off limits for youngsters?"

"Not at all," Liam turned to Charlie. "I'm sure you and your sister will not try climbing down the roof from the third-floor balcony."

"You did what?" Charlie exclaimed. "Wow! No way! That's super high."

"Don't give them any ideas!" Nora said with a shocked expression on her face.

Liam cast his eyes down to hide his grin. "Let's just say I pushed my grandmother's limits a few too many times over the years."

"I'll ask her about that when we talk later. I hear your adventuring into the underwater world around this area."

"You're what?" Charlie asked.

"Yes, I'm scuba diving to explore several of the shipwrecks in this lake. I love taking photographs of them. In fact, I was on a dive yesterday."

"Really? That's so cool. I'd love to do that. Tell me what it's like."

"Well Charlie, how about we talk on our way up toward the Fort's entrance?" Liam said as he put his arm around Charlie's shoulder and started walking up the path to Fort Mackinac.

13

LILLIA

I heard Liam telling Charlie, "You'd be surprised at how well preserved some shipwrecks are, mainly because the waters are so cold here. Sometimes Lake Huron freezes over and people are allowed to take snowmobiles over to the island because the boats can't get through."

Charlie said, "We heard about that on the tour. Pretty crazy! What ship did you see yesterday?"

"We dived to the Sandusky. It's the oldest known wreck in this area."

I found the idea of seeing old ships down there under the water pretty interesting too. Almost like old abandoned houses. "What happened to it?"

"A violent storm sprang up catching the Sandusky in the Straits of Mackinac in the fall of 1856. These waters can be very treacherous, especially when gale force winds blow through. Reports from that time recorded that a steamship tried to rescue the crew who climbed the masts as the ship was sinking," Liam said.

Grauntie Nora joined in with a question. "Did they save the crew?"

Liam shook his head.

"That's so sad," Grauntie said. "Were there passengers onboard too?"

"No, this was a merchant vessel, brig type, traveling from Chicago with a load of grain."

"So, you dove down and saw a ship lying on the bottom of the lake that sunk over one hundred years ago?" I said, trying to imagine what that would look like. What it would feel like to be swimming around it?

"Yep, and I'm going back tomorrow."

"How fun. But I thought you were going to be here on the island overnight," Grauntie said, the disappointment evident in her voice.

"Sorry, I was planning on that. But a storm is moving in faster than expected and the dive crew has scheduled another dive to the Sandusky for tomorrow. Otherwise it'll be days before the waters settle down again. I will be back to see you right afterward."

I was curious. "Why are you going back down so soon again?"

"Well…a little something seemed to be lurking in the murky waters nearby."

"A pirate ship?" Charlie shouted excitedly.

Liam held up his hands as we arrived at the entrance to the fort sitting high above the park and the shoreline. "I don't think there were pirates on the Great Lakes. I'll let you know more after tomorrow's dive. But first I insist on showing you the oldest public building in the whole state of Michigan, the Officer's Stone Quarters." He winked at Charlie. "And it happens there is a restaurant inside of it. I'll treat us all to lunch. How's that sound Charlie?"

I watched my brother give Liam a fist bump. "But later the story about what you saw?"

"You got it," Liam answered.

I was glad to hear the word lunch. Hunger pangs hit me just as we turned the corner and the smell of food floated out to us. On the outdoor terrace each table held a bright yellow umbrella. The effect was like entering a field of giant sunflowers.

"This view is out of this world," Grauntie said. "The perfect spot for lunch on the island. Thank you for bringing us here."

After we'd ordered our lunch I asked, "Did you ever finish that story you were working on at the writer retreat in the Superstition Wilderness?"

"I'm wrapping it up now and getting ready to send it to my editor. That retreat turned out to be quite the experience."

"You've got that right. I still find it hard to believe someone would go to those lengths to ruin a family's reputation. And for what?" I said.

"Well they say there's a Curse of the Superstitions. That might have had something to do with it," Liam said. "Stranger things have happened. At least you exposed the culprit."

I blushed at the compliment...my imagining abilities did help out, so I had an advantage. "Liam, I'm puzzled. Why did your grandpa call this Mystery Island?"

"Grandpa Schmidt always liked the idea of having a home on an island. Taking the ferry and then a horse drawn carriage to get to the house, meant stepping back in time for him. He said the island felt mysterious. Like someone from the past could be sticking around fitting in with life here."

Grauntie asked him if he knew much about the past history of the Pelletier house.

"To be honest, that never really interested me. I was always off exploring, biking, fishing, horseback riding. Outdoor stuff. The waters here have always intrigued me. It's the reason I got my scuba diving certification."

"Hey, you promised you'd tell us what you photographed!" Charlie said.

"You're right. I did. I think I may have seen another wreck while we were exploring the Sandusky."

"So? I heard there are lots of wrecks out there," Charlie said. "Why would that be a big deal?"

Liam replied, "What makes it a big deal is there has not been another wreck discovered in that area…ever!"

14

MYSTERY SHIPWRECK

Liam could tell Charlie was surprised. So was Lillia. So am I he thought. Showing them the fort would be a good distraction to get that next dive off his mind. He didn't want to expect too much. After all, how often was a new wreck discovered? Like almost never!

Grauntie, in her usual manner, took time to read all the descriptive placards, while Liam kept Charlie and Lillia entertained showing them around Fort Mackinac. Lillia enjoyed seeing the rooms, furnished with period pieces, where the soldiers and their families had lived.

The afternoon was going by fast and Liam still had other places he wanted them to see. But before they left, he gathered them all together around a cannon. They watched and listened as the reenactment soldiers explained how the cannon was cleaned, loaded, primed, and readied for ignition. Then, to Charlie's surprise, he was picked to pull the rope that fired the cannon!

"Wow! That was cool," Charlie said. "I can't wait to tell Mom and Dad that I fired a real cannon."

"Glad you got to do it," Liam said as he led them out of the fort and down to the park.

When Grauntie saw the name of the park was Marquette, she told Liam about meeting the Canadian couple who were following the Marquette and Joliet Trail.

"Canadians are such friendly people," Liam said. "One of the things Louis Joliet was involved in, when he wasn't exploring, was the fur trade. That business dominated life on this island for many years. I want to show you the American Fur Company Store," Liam said. "John Jacob Astor owned it. He grew his businesses to become one of the richest men in America. This island is where he got his start. Right this way."

Liam led them to a white stone building at the edge of the park. "We're on the appropriately named Market Street. This was the main supply store for the island during the busiest days of the fur trade."

"We heard that the Pelletiers were in that business too," Lillia said.

"They were. So many trappers brought their furs here that both families did well. The store exhibits merchandise available to the traders and the trappers. That time was a period of growth for the area. The Dr. Beaumont Museum is in the same building. Come on let me show you…it's pretty amazing what happened right here on Mackinac Island."

The story of the young man who was accidentally shot in the stomach in the American Fur Store captured their attention. Liam explained that Dr. Beaumont saved the man's life, but the procedure left him with an unhealed, permanent opening in his stomach. Through that wound gap that didn't close up, Dr. Beaumont was given a pathway to study the human digestive process.

"Dr. Beaumont later wrote a groundbreaking book on the subject. Pretty neat huh?" Liam asked Charlie, who was looking just a bit pale. "Looks like this is a bit too graphic for you. How about we hit up the stores and find us some fudge?"

Grauntie agreed with Liam's idea. "We can't miss that!"

After strolling the Main Street, browsing in fudge and gift shops, Grauntie suggested it might be time for dinner. "I'd like to treat you this time Liam. I know you want to leave to return to St. Ignace soon, so is there something right downtown here that you could suggest?"

"I highly recommend the Lakeshore Cafe. It's a local joint where you'll meet some of the people who live here on the island. They have photos of shipwrecks on their walls and I'm sure Charlie would get a kick out of that," Liam said.

As soon as the group walked in, a waitress came up and gave Liam a big hug. "Hey there Liam. Long time no see. And who's this handsome young man and lovely young lady you have with you?"

"Sherry, I'd like you to meet the Pameroys. They are staying at Grandma's house for a couple of days."

"Welcome to the Lakeshore Cafe! By the way, where are your grandparents? Haven't seen much of them this summer."

"Grandma's hip has been giving her a lot of trouble."

"Oh no. I remember she was bothered by that last summer. Well you be sure to give her my best. She's such a sweetie. Follow me, only the best table in the house for you and your guests. Right here by the window."

"Thanks Sherry," Liam said.

Charlie got up to walk around and look at photographs of shipwrecks hanging on the walls.

"Impressive isn't it?" Liam asked as he walked up behind Charlie. "The ship in that photo is the Eber Ward."

"Looks like it's just sitting there straight up on the bottom of the lake," Charlie said. "Have you dived to see it?"

"Yes, I have. The ship's captain thought they were just running through a field of slush, so no big deal. But turns out it was thick, deep ice and it tore the bow open, sinking the ship right straight down. It was a deep dive for us, but once we were down that deep, we didn't have to fight currents which was nice."

"Maybe I'll do that someday. Can I see the photos you took?"

"First, let me show you the photographs hanging on the walls here."

They crossed to the back wall. "This is the Sandusky wreck, the one I just dove to. My photos aren't as good as these. And here is what it looked like before."

Charlie stood on his tiptoes. "Cool, like a pirate ship! All those big sails. Did it hit ice too?"

"Nope, she got caught in a violent gale. Around here we can get hurricane like winds and over thirty-foot waves. Nowadays there's much better communication about storms in the area, still the sinking of the Edmund Fitzgerald happened in just 1975. That was one of the largest shipwrecks on the lakes…took the lives of thirty-three crew members."

Liam pointed to a collage of underwater photos. "This was identified as the St. Andrew. It collided with another ship, the Peshtigo, in 1857 and they both sank. But weird story, the Peshtigo has never been found."

"So how can that be? How do they know it sank?"

"Some of the crew survived. It was long ago so information sharing was different then. But Charlie, something pretty exciting happened last month. A local explorer has positively identified a wreck fifty miles away as being those two ships, the Peshtigo and the St. Andrew. Can you believe it? It was far away in Lake Michigan not Lake Huron and both ships are there... right next to each other."

"What is this wreck then?" Charlie asked, pointing back to the photograph in front of them.

"That's what they'll have to go back and figure out. There's a volunteer group that runs the Straits of Mackinac Shipwreck Preserve. They map and mark the wreck sites for divers. I'm sure it'll get figured out. New photos will be going up on these walls soon."

"Why don't you write a mystery novel about it?"

Liam thought a moment. "You know, that's not a bad idea. But first I want to discover what I saw when we dove to the Sandusky yesterday. Looks like our food is here buddy. Let's go eat!"

Liam's phone with the underwater photos he took was passed around the table several times. Sherry stopped by to see his underwater photos too.

"Well look at this. I sure think there's something in

those murky waters. I can feel it. I consider myself very receptive and open to things like that," she said.

Liam said, "Really Sherry? That's interesting. My friend texted these to me. I left my camera with her. The originals are being uploaded and looked at back in the dive shop."

Grauntie said, "I'm afraid I don't have Sherry's sensibilities. I just don't see anything."

"Hopefully the next time we get together I'll have better photos. And maybe I'll even be able to claim I discovered a new wreck!" Liam said, the anticipation in his voice was evident to those around him.

Sherry giggled. "Ooops! I didn't mean that to come out. Sorry, but Liam, the odds of you finding another wreck are slim."

Charlie piped up. "A diver found those two ships from almost a hundred and fifty years ago."

"What? A new wreck found?" Sherry just shook her head. "Well slap me upside my big mouth. You go Liam. You find it!"

"And you even thought you saw something in my photo Sherry, right?" Liam asked.

"That I did. But I was talking about capturing the image of a ghost ship."

15

LILLIA

My ears perked up at that comment. A ghost ship? Interesting. I looked carefully at the waitress standing by our table. Did I sense we might have something in common?

"Sherry, you and your ghosts." Liam laughed. "You and Grandma would always try telling me there was a ghost in the attic at the house. If you were trying to scare me away from it, I can tell you it only made me more curious to go up there!"

"You were quite the adventuresome young boy," Sherry said. "It's not just me who thinks that house is haunted. Young folk like Liam here just dismiss all that sort of stuff. They don't know."

"My Lillia here has a thing for ghosts too. Don't you Lillia?" Grauntie gave me a wink.

Sherry turned her gaze toward me. I couldn't look

away. An awkward silence hung between us. No one at the table spoke for several seconds. Sherry cleared her throat. "Is that so? Perhaps we're kindred spirits then? Best you go up to the attic and check it out then Lillia. See what you can come up with."

Almost involuntarily I nodded. There was something about her. An aura. I noticed Charlie shifting in his seat at the direction the conversation was going.

I was glad to hear Sherry say, "Back to work for me. You be careful out there tomorrow Liam. That storm's moving mighty fast."

"I'll be sure to let you know if it's only a ghost ship Sherry," Liam said.

The gangway for passengers to board the ferry was being pulled up, but Liam called out for them to wait. The crew paused the operation so Liam could get onboard.

Liam shouted, "See you all soon. Hopefully tomorrow! Be sure..." The ship's horn blasted, and we didn't hear the rest of his words. But he kept waving until the ferry passed out of sight behind the buildings on the pier.

I was ready to get home, it had been a long day. The carriage ride, lunch at the fort, and all the other sights. I was beat.

As we walked past the last buildings of the downtown area, we saw Liam's ferry lights in the distance...small, far away. A strange feeling passed through me. A lonely isolated feeling.

The island was softening into twilight, the dimming time. Lights at the Grand Hotel were coming on. A carriage rolled past us with its coach lights lit, the couple inside all dressed up for dinner. As Grauntie turned to walk up the hill, Charlie asked if we could take the beach back.

"Charlie, I don't know if I can take the steep walk back up to those stairs from the beach. This gentle slope is better for me this time of night. How about you two walk the beach from here and I'll meet you back at the house?"

"I'm tired too. Can't we just go tomorrow?" I asked Charlie.

"Please Lillia. Come with me." He tried tempting me. "We could look for sea glass."

"Probably too dark for that," Grauntie said.

Taking a quick look for sea glass was tempting. I shrugged, willing to give it a try. "Okay, I'll go. But you owe me one little brother."

"See you back at the house. Don't dawdle," Grauntie said.

My eyes got used the darkness once we were away from the town lights.

"Do you think Liam will be okay diving tomorrow?" Charlie asked. A tone of genuine concern in his question.

"I suppose they watch the weather really close so everyone's safe."

"Wouldn't it be cool to do that? Swim down and look in the windows of an old shipwreck? Pretty crazy how you're sailing along on top of a lake and then bam... down you go."

I shook my head. "Charlie, really. It's an awful thing that happened to those ships. The people that drowned. Not everyone gets out of a sinking ship safely."

"I know. Liam told me that. Do you think they ever find bones when they go diving?"

"I don't even want to think about that. But I doubt it. Those wrecks are so old."

"I heard about how sailors bury people at sea. Just wrap 'em up and..."

"Charlie, stop right now!" I was regretting giving in to his idea of a walk on the beach. But he didn't hear me as he yelped and ran up ahead.

Charlie bent down and picked something up, waving it above his head. The wind carried his whoops back to me. I couldn't make out what it was he had found.

16

STRANGE FEELINGS

Sherry noticed Nora and the two kids walk back past the diner after they dropped Liam at the ferry. Looked like they were on their way back to the Pelletier house. Probably was best that she didn't get time to tell them the stories she'd heard about the house. The boy didn't like talk of ghosts. But that girl, what was her name? There was something different about her.

The old man in the corner, always the last to leave, was neatly folding his paper napkin and placing his coffee cup atop it. He lined up the spoon just so and pushed back from the table. "Looks like it's gettin' time for me to leave Sherry. You'll be wanting to close up."

Sherry nodded. "Looking forward to putting my feet up that's for sure."

"I overheard a bit of what that young man was

talking about. Hope he finds what he's looking for. Couldn't drag me down into those dark waters for love or money. Sounds mighty dangerous."

Sherry walked to the diner door and stepped outside. "I agree. But it sounds sort of wonderfully mysterious too. Maybe the currents shifted something around down there and it is an undiscovered wreck. He'll know tomorrow."

"Might be that," the man said. "Might be he was just seeing an illusion. Or like you said, one of the spirit ships."

Sherry chuckled as she looked up at the night sky. "Starting to feel like that storm. The older I get the better my bones are with weather predictions."

"He a local boy?"

"Liam's grandparents are Dorothy and Edgar Schmidt. They own the Pelletier house. He comes most every summer to stay with them. Those family friends he was with are staying in the house a few days." Sherry leaned in toward the old man. "I suspect you've heard about that place?"

"Can't say I have. One of those mansions they like to call cottages?"

"Yes. The place is haunted. The old lady that died there is hanging around for some reason. Like a spirit who isn't ready to leave."

The old man looked surprised. "Is that so? Wonder what she wants."

Sherry laughed. "Well I have no idea. But I hope she gets it! Goodnight now."

"Night Sherry."

"Take care walking home."

Then it came to her. Lillia. Her name was Lillia.

The door flew open and Nora watched Charlie come running in with Lillia right behind.

Charlie waved something in front of his Grauntie Nora's face. "We found a bottle on the beach!"

Nora stepped back. "Slow down. Don't hit me with it. A glass bottle you say?" She reached to take it from him.

"And it looks like there's something in it," Lillia added with excitement.

"It sure does. Looks really old too."

Charlie grabbed it back from her. "The top is rusted and we couldn't get it off, but I'm going to put some cooking oil on to loosen it. Do you think that'll work?"

Grauntie's face took on a puzzled look. "Hmm…it might. Would be better than breaking it open I suppose."

Charlie took off for the kitchen with the bottle grasped against his chest.

"Oh, and I got information on the attic for you Lillia. Just finished talking with Dorothy," Grauntie said.

"So, I can go up there tonight?"

"Sure. She wasn't certain if the lights still work though. Apparently when they bought this house, they left most everything the way it was. For decades only Clarisse lived here."

"That's a neat name. Who was she?"

Grauntie said, "Let's sit out on the porch and I'll tell you everything Dorothy told me."

As they watched the stars come out from the comfort of wicker chairs, Grauntie Nora shared the brief history Dorothy had given her. The Schmidts bought the house on a whim. As a summer place for their family to enjoy. "She told me that it seemed like the spirit of the house was alive in all the things left in it. Clarisse was a Pelletier and she left gorgeous furniture, dishware, and linens to be sold with the house. So why change them?"

"The house sits empty all winter?" Lillia asked.

"Yes. Not many people stay for the winter. Even the majority of the horses are taken back to the mainland. But in her humorous way Dorothy continued her story, telling me this house didn't truly remain empty when they left. Apparently, it has a resident ghost!"

Lillia's eyes lit up. "Really? That's what Sherry at the diner was suggesting. So that's who I heard walking around?"

"You know, I bet it could be," Grauntie Nora replied with a wink.

"What made her think there was a ghost?"

She talked about a few things that happened here. Like when they returned one summer, furniture was rearranged. Objects would be found in unusual spots, and no one seemed to know how they got there. A few times, when they were on the ferry, they thought they saw someone on the third-floor balcony."

"That's what happened today on the tour!"

Grauntie nodded. "I remember that. Dorothy took it for granted that such a special old home would have a ghost or two. It never concerned or bothered her she said. I think she kind of got a kick out it. Something to tell visitors about."

"What was it about the attic though? Why did they lock it? Because of Liam?"

Grauntie Nora laughed and slapped her leg. "It was exactly as Liam said! To keep a curious young boy out of trouble. Afterward Dorothy never bothered going up there. She told me walking up one flight of stairs to get to her bedroom was quite enough for a lady with a bad hip."

17

LILLIA

.

"Did she tell you where we can find the key?" I was now super excited to get to the attic. Would I find what had caused the *tap tap tap* sound? In my gut I knew it wasn't a raccoon.

"The key is on top of the door frame up there. I can help you get it later."

Charlie came walking in all pouty faced. "I can't get this thing open."

"Be careful Charlie. It might be from some old war. Maybe there's poisonous gas in it. When you open it, you could put us all in danger!" I said running up to grab it from him.

"Grauntie, make her stop."

"Lillia, give him the bottle back. Come on Charlie, let's go see if we have a tool that might open it."

"First me Grauntie. Remember? The attic key?"

"Ah yes. Hang on, I'll be right back with you Charlie." Grauntie took the bottle from my hands and gave it to Charlie. "It's such a dark blue color that you can't even see inside."

Charlie shook it. "Hear that? It sounds like a piece of metal. Maybe a gold coin!"

I thought yeah sure. He always likes to think he will find treasure. In Alabama, Charlie got in trouble over his search for it. I had to rescue him. At least with this treasure the worst he'll get is a cut from broken glass.

Grauntie climbed the two flights of stairs ahead of me and reached to retrieve the key from the door jamb ledge. She unlocked the door and flipped a switch. "No animals, but no working lights either. Do you want to wait until morning Lillia?"

"No. Maybe I can find a flashlight downstairs to use."

About ten minutes later I was back at the door with a flashlight, ready to see what was in this place.

Straight ahead the beam bounced back at me, probably from a window across on the other side. There was a lot of darkness between me and that window. The place smelled closed off. It had been locked up for years according to the stories I'd heard.

A small hallway was off to my left. With hesitancy, I opened the first door. It contained that pungent smell of moth balls I remembered from that Wisconsin mansion's attic. This isn't where I'd heard the footsteps coming from. It was only a large closet.

The next door revealed a modest sized room. Through a dormer window I could see the soft lighting of the Grand Hotel. I scanned my flashlight beam around the rest of the room. It held a bed with a quilt spread across it and a pillow resting against the white enamel headboard. A nightstand held a lamp, two books, and a cup. In the corner under the eaves sat a dresser with a lace scarf covering the top. I walked over to look more closely at what it held. There were three photographs in frames, a tiny lidded container, an empty single bud vase, and a hairbrush. The photographs were of a family group, a large sail ship, and an older couple.

Could this have been a room for a maid or cook? Or maybe a nanny?

I wanted to find that balcony we'd seen from the carriage tour this morning. The one someone stood on. It had to be off of the room ahead.

I passed through the space with my flashlight beam moving back and forth slowly in front of me. No good to trip on something. Grauntie and Charlie were two floors below me and wouldn't hear me.

My first impression was that this had been a play-room for the Pelletier children. A big wooden rocking horse was tucked in one corner. Its finish dull and chipped. The yarn mane twisted and tangled around its sad looking face. A broken-backed chair leaned down against a child-size table holding books.

Suddenly my feet got caught up in a small throw rug and the flashlight flew out of my hand. Rolling away, dizzily spinning, coming to a stop shining on a pair of shoes with pants legs rising up from them!

I lay as still as my nerves would allow. Were those the shoes making the sounds last night?

They didn't move.

I didn't move.

Someone had to move.

I took a shallow breath and got to my hands and knees.

The legs didn't move.

I stood up in a crouch, loose, ready to spring and run. The flashlight taunted me…just out of reach. I moved in a low squat, shuffling toward the flashlight.

I picked it up. It felt good. Weighty. A weapon.

I kept the beam aimed toward the shoes.

Those aren't real shoes at all!

I stood upright to take in what I was looking at. The life size painting of a man in a gilded frame, leaning against the wall.

Scolding myself for being so stupid but grateful no

one was around to witness it, I breathed a sigh of relief. Next to the man's portrait was one of a woman in a beautiful blue gown. Those sure didn't fit in a child's playroom.

Now back to finding that balcony. I was more careful to pay attention to where I walked. The balcony door was at the furthest end of the room, next to windows that had reflected my flashlight beam. It opened easily.

Cool night air flowed into the room and so did the giggles of a young child.

18

THE DIVE SHOP

Liam hurried from St. Ignace's ferry dock to Joe's Dive Shop. He hoped they'd still be open. He'd left his underwater camera with Abby, who was both his dive partner and a computer genius, to download the photos from yesterday. He was excited to see what they looked like on a big screen instead of just his cellphone. He headed to the back office.

"Good trip to the island?" Abby asked.

"It was. I did the usual tourist stuff with Grandma's friends. Beautiful day for it. Then grabbed dinner with them at the Lakeshore Cafe."

"Is Sherry still working there?"

"She is."

Abby laughed. "She's like an institution. Almost a

tourist attraction in her own right. Did you get the photos I sent to your phone?"

"I did. Thanks Abby. Were you able to see anything unusual in them?"

"They weren't taken at a very high resolution. When we go back to the wreck site tomorrow be sure the resolution settings are at the highest they can be. Whatever additional shots you get we can enlarge them to the maximum."

"Okay, I'll be sure to do that," Liam said.

Abby turned back to the computer screen and Liam leaned in over her shoulder to watch. The images he'd shown everyone just a couple of hours ago at the Lakeshore Cafe were up on the screen. He saw them with much more clarity in this large format.

"I wasn't able to blow them up very much without a lot of distortion," Abby said, pointing at the photos. "But as you can see there does appear to be something deep in the background. But it could be so many things. Even a shadow from the surface."

Liam looked it over carefully. Had he been fooled? It sure didn't look like what he'd seen with his own eyes. "Not much to go on huh?"

"We trust your instincts Liam and we'll do another dive. If it is a previously unidentified wreck, it would be quite a find. But that would probably mean it was never discovered because it was buried in silt or had shifted with the currents. We want to try to find it before this storm comes and risks it being hidden again."

Abby rose from her desk chair and stretched. "I'm calling it a night. The boat is leaving super early in the morning to get ahead of the storm. It took some convincing to get Joe to authorize it. The reports are that this storm is a big one."

19

LILLIA

I gasped. For a second I thought the childish giggles came from behind me. Or were they outside? They seemed to be everywhere. Soft. Low. Melodic. All around me.

The balcony was barely big enough for someone to stand on. I leaned over the side to see if someone was outside. But what kid would be out at this time of night? It was too dark to see anything on the ground two floors down.

Come play with me…giggles…

I spun, shining my light into the room's darkness.

A lamp switched on! Its soft glow casting a cone of light downward. I lowered the flashlight to my side.

A man and a woman appeared. They sat in armchairs, one on either side of the lamp. They held hands, reaching across the space between them where a child sat on the floor.

Mommy. Daddy. Don't go. I want to play more.

The man and woman don't answer her. They smile at the child as she stands and looks at me. I'm frozen to the spot.

Behind her I see the wooden rocking horse...now a proud arch to its neck. A braided yarn mane cascades down. The body glossy and smooth in the lamp light.

Will you play with me?

As I step from the balcony and back into the room, the couple rise and walk toward the large portrait paintings. They step into the frames...out of the room.

The horse begins to rock. The child's tiny fingers hug the yarn mane. She pulls herself up on it. Her eyes stare at me as she lays herself down on the wooden neck of her rocking horse.

They never came back. Promise you will come back.

The horse rocks slowly. The lamp light snaps off. She is gone.

With the flashlight beam pointed at the floor I whisper, *I will. I promise.*

20

STORM WARNINGS

Morning on Mackinac Island found Sherry once again at work in the Lakeshore Cafe. The long days were getting hard on her. But it was summer and the busiest time here. Come fall, things start quieting…and then winter comes, and it was only locals she'd see.

Those nice people staying at the Pelletier house were in again this morning. "Good morning all! What are you having today?" Sherry asked, pen poised above the small ordering pad in her hand.

"Pancakes for that one," Nora said, her head tipping toward Charlie who wandered off to look at the photos again. "I'll have the bacon and egg plate. Coffee too please."

"And you young lady?"

"I'll do a waffle and orange juice," Lillia answered.

"What are your plans for today?"

"We're going to do the bike ride around the whole island," Nora said.

A young woman at the next table leaned over. "Be sure to go clockwise. You'll be on the other side of the island when the gusts get stronger. We did it yesterday and it was pretty easy, but with the storm coming the winds will be picking up." Sherry nodded. "She's right. Some of the bigger tankers have already pulled into safe harbors instead of trying to make it across the lakes. We'll be seeing more and more anchoring in here as the day goes on. Mainly pleasure boats though I suspect."

A few minutes later, when Sherry arrived with their plates of food, Charlie came hurrying back to the table to dig into his stack of pancakes.

"Saw you studying the shipwreck photos," the young woman said. "Do you like ships? I do!"

Charlie smiled at her. "I guess I do. My dad and I like to fish from our small boat. The ferry ride over here was fun. But I've never been on a really big ship."

"You did the Captain Jack's Pirate Cruise," Lillia reminded him.

"That's right. That was a big ship with sails. It was fun too," Charlie said.

"Do you think the storm will be really bad?" Grauntie asked.

"That's what I heard," the young woman said. "I'm just a tourist here too. We were hoping to do the carriage tour today."

Sherry said, "You should be fine with that, you're not exposed to the wind as much as riding the perimeter road. Charlie, some folks around here say that when a bad storm comes blowing through, some of those very vessels you see in the shipwreck photos, will sail into this harbor trying to reach shelter. The spirit ships they call them."

Charlie nervously asked, "Is this storm going to be so bad that those spirit ships show up?"

Oops, Sherry thought. Forgot about his being a little skittish about ghosts and stuff. Glad I don't feel uneasy about them. Goodness knows they're all around us, especially in a place like Mackinac Island.

Grauntie Nora, quick to offer a distraction said, "Sherry, do you know how to get a rusty old cap off a bottle without breaking it?"

Sherry laughed. "If it's that old and rusty I'd throw it out!"

Charlie, who's attention was taken from ghost ships to treasure in a bottle, "But I found a bottle washed up on the shore. There's something in it. I shake it and it rattles. The glass is too dark to see through."

Nodding sagely Sherry said, "Smart move to keep it intact. Let me think on that."

"Come on Charlie. Let Sherry get back to work. We need to finish up our breakfast so we can get on with our bike ride."

The woman at the next table leaned over again and suggested a special oil to loosen the top. "The local hardware store might carry it," she said.

"Why thank you. We'll be sure to pick some up when we get back from our ride," Nora said.

After the Pameroys finished breakfast and left the restaurant, the customer said, "Those people were nice. Hope they have a fun bike ride. Sherry, is that story true about the ghost ships? I like paranormal stuff."

"Oh my, so do I. I've never seen one of the spirit ships, but I've talked to people who claim they have."

"That's neat. Do you know any other ghost stories about the island?"

"The very house those three people are staying in is haunted. Scoot over, I'll tell you a bit about it."

The young woman was all wide-eyed and eager to hear the tale of Clarisse Pelletier that Sherry proceeded to share with her. She finished the story by saying, "Poor old gal. Went a little looney I think. All those long winters by herself. Too much time to think about losing her parents like that."

21

LILLIA

I hadn't slept well last night. Who was that child? She must be a Pelletier. But what happened to her parents? Was she the ghost Sherry and Dorothy thought lived in the house?

Setting out from the bike rental shop we headed past the fudge shops of downtown, past the Lakeshore Cafe, and along the shoreline road. I kept my eye on the third-floor balcony of our house as we passed. But no one appeared up there today.

"Hey, watch where you're going!" Charlie swerved away quickly, or I would have run into him.

"Better pay attention to what you're doing Lillia. I don't need one of you to take a tumble," Grauntie said.

She was right. I'd enjoy this ride today, but tonight

I'm back up in those rooms. After all, I keep my promises.

I turned my attention back to the bike ride. This is crazy nice! Nothing like our bike paths back home in Kansas. We were on a road! With no cars!

Ahead of me Charlie was taking advantage of the situation by weaving and crisscrossing over the roadway. We hadn't seen anyone else biking yet either.

Grauntie came up behind me. "What were you staring at?"

"I was just remembering last night in the third floor. It had little a closet, a small bedroom, and a nice big playroom. I was just thinking about who might have used it."

"You have a great imagination," Grauntie Nora said with a knowing grin. "I'll bet you'll figure it out before we leave in a couple of days. Maybe you'll discover that ghost Dorothy thinks still lives in the house. You'll be sure to let me know?"

Grauntie knew about my special imagining abilities, but she didn't push me about them. She knew she could trust my instincts to not walk into anything dangerous or do anything stupid. Though there was that time during a snowstorm in a cave high up on Whistler's Ridge. Oh yeah and facing the angry Pirate Queen in the Alabama backwaters. And then that house crashing in around me during a thunderstorm in

Kentucky. Sometimes you just have to act I keep telling myself.

"I know. I know. You'll tell me about it on the way home, right?" Grauntie said with a funny grin. "Same line all the time."

She and I can kid about that line I use, but I usually do tell her after it's over. I gave her a quick thumbs up as she rode by me. She was trying to catch Charlie from pedaling past the first stop she wanted us to see. It was a sea cave carved in limestone…Devil's Kitchen.

"It was formed about 350 million years ago the sign says. Yikes that's old!" Charlie told Grauntie and me as we caught up with him. "It says the soft parts were eroded by wave action from the lake over decades."

Grauntie looked at the large rock that sat right at the edge of the road. "I didn't realize that lake waves can push up over this road. We better keep going. I don't want to end up pedaling through water! This storm is pushing in toward the island. By the evening those little waves will be whitecaps."

I stopped to straddle my bike and look out across the lake. In the far distance, what looked at first glance like a dark gray line of hills or low mountains, was really the faint outline of a bank of clouds. Bright sunshine still shone on the lake's surface, but the wind was already making each ripple in the surface deeper. I couldn't avoid the slightly ominous sense I got. I happen to love a good storm, if I'm safe inside of course.

The rocky beach continued on our left as we rode along the island's edge. Eventually the tree covered bluffs were broken by a set of beach stairs to some unseen house. Then a couple of driveways left the road, or here are they called carriageways? Soon the steepness of the land rising beside us lowered. We peeked through the trees and saw a few houses right at shore level.

The first people we'd seen since starting out this morning, a group of six bikers, were stopped by another roadside sign up ahead.

Charlie was excited when he read it, because it pointed out the way to Skull Cave. "Let's go check that out," he said, already turning his bike away from the shoreline road.

"Hold on buddy. I don't think that's a good idea. I know it's not far, but I don't like the look of the sky and we're not even halfway around yet."

"But Skull Cave! Come on Grauntie, how can you not want to see that?"

"I know, I know, but we can't do everything. Let's keep going."

My hair whipped around my face now. I was getting tired of pedaling and fighting the wind. The sharpness of the air pushing against me stung my skin. I'd end up with both windburn and sunburn.

Grauntie looked like she was struggling too. She stopped to catch her breath. "We're almost to the northern point of the island. We should be more sheltered from this wind once we make the turn."

She was right. Soon as we rounded the northerly point we rode in relative calm. We climbed slightly higher, the edge of the road now steep cliffs dropping away to the lake. A nice coast downhill and our road went back to lake level.

The Arch Rock appeared. It looked so different from this point of view. Hikers, who'd walked down a steep set of stairs from the top of the bluff, stood on the road looking back up at the rock.

One pleasant looking woman asked me how the bike ride was.

"Really pretty. And easy, except the wind's been getting stronger on the other side. Here it's not so bad. Are we almost back to town?" Grauntie asked.

"Yes, it's not far. From alerts I've been hearing, the storm is moving much faster than expected. Once you make the turn into the harbor area, I'm sure you'll feel it again."

And she was right...the wind hit us hard as we entered the harbor area!

22

SAFE HARBOR

Ever since the breakwater was installed to protect the harbor on Mackinac Island, ships have come in for shelter before a storm hits. Today was no different. Sail boats anchored off. Boat slips were filled. The hotels were busy with the boat owners booking rooms for the night.

The usually pleasant, melodic harbor sound provided by the gentle clanging of sailing vessels rigging was gone. Now the sharp winds slapping at the rigging created a harsh and strident noise that could be heard across the small town huddled on the hill.

Ferry companies, knowing that they would not be able to run on their regular schedule today, shuttled as many passengers as they could to fill the demand to get off the island before the storm hit.

All the yellow umbrellas at the Tea Room restaurant

high above the town were closed up and taken down. People on the broad greens of Marquette Square were staring out toward the slate gray clouds pushing in. Fudge shop windows were being boarded up. Warning announcements broadcasted loudly through the town. White caps crashed against the breakwater.

"Glad to see you three back safe and sound. We stopped renting out bikes shortly after you left. This storm is moving like a freight train and it's headed right for us," the manager of the bicycle shop said.

"So are we. I had no idea this was so close, or I wouldn't have taken these two out," Grauntie Nora said.

"Its speed and strength are catching us all by surprise ma'am."

"Do you think Liam will catch a ferry returning today?" Charlie asked.

"I don't know," Grauntie said. "I just hope they aren't still out there diving trying to find that phantom shipwreck."

"These storms tend to kick up all sorts of surprises from the bottom of the lake," the bike guy said, handing Grauntie her receipt. "Here you go."

"We enjoyed the ride. This is a beautiful island, but I think it's time we head back to the house where we can watch the storm's arrival from the shelter of our porch."

"Sounds like a good idea. I'm closing up my shop right behind you."

* * *

The dive boat was rocking wildly in the waves. Totally caught off guard by the speed of the approaching storm, the captain was kicking himself for even agreeing to take the group out today.

He'd tied down all the equipment and gear, readying the ship to return to St. Ignace.

"Everyone up?" he asked the dive leader.

A quick count showed they were missing two divers…Liam and Abby.

"Get them up right now! It's getting too rough out here for my comfort. I thought you gave the signal awhile go."

"The divers were given the alarm to get topside as soon as possible and we all did." The leader watched for them to appear by the mooring line that guided divers back up. "I know they saw the signal."

Deep in the depths of Lake Huron, far below the dive boat, Liam felt his dive buddy Abby tapping him. Gesturing. Pointing up. Signaling they needed to get to the surface stat.

The other divers had adjusted their buoyancy

compensators, which allowed them to rise up to the boat, minutes ago. They were all out of sight.

Liam shook his head side to side. He held up one finger and pointed toward his underwater camera. He knew he had to swim just a few feet more. He had to capture an image of what he glimpsed a few seconds ago.

Abby's eyes behind her full-face mask pleaded with Liam. He couldn't avoid the panic he saw in them and the message that they had to go now. He knew that dive buddies were supposed to stay together for safety reasons. She had to go. He didn't want to put her in danger., but he couldn't leave. He must make one more attempt to capture a photo of what he'd seen.

Breaking away from Abby as she grabbed at him, Liam kicked hard with his flippers propelling himself toward the wreck and away from safety. Away from Abby.

Then there it was. Looming out of the murky water in front of him. It took his breath away. Even in these deep cold depths, the beauty of the carved figurehead was breathtaking. The detailed, ornate figurehead of a sailing vessel that had never been discovered before. He snapped a few shots then spun to race back to the dive boat.

But where was he? Where was the mooring line to guide him back up? He started breathing too fast. Sucking in too much air from his tank. His frightened eyes wide open behind his face mask.

23

LILLIA

The air felt different to me now. I'd learned in science class about weather and air pressure, so I understood that part. But beyond that there was a pulsing sensation…like I was feeling the earth's powerful heart beating.

I was snapped out of my idiotic poetic stupor by Charlie pushing past me. I grimaced as he bolted sideways off the sidewalk startling a horse. The giant tried rearing up, but the harness restrained him.

"Sorry," Charlie yelled back at the carriage driver as he raced away.

Grauntie Nora took time to stop and apologize too.

The driver looked down from his seat and said, "These horses are used to kids running out in front of them. I'm just shocked she startled like that. Guess even the horses are affected by this arriving storm."

I figured Charlie was on his way to the small hardware store to check for that special oil to get that rusted cap off the blue bottle.

Grauntie said, "I might as well get light bulbs for the third floor while we're here. That's probably all that's needed to give you light to explore by."

I waited outside while Grauntie went in the store. Then, out of the blue, Henry Thatcher hurried by on the other side of the street. I called out to him. He spun to look around. He seemed confused. Frantic.

I waved high above my head. "Here Henry, by the hardware store." I think my voice was carried off by the wind because he still didn't see me.

He almost lost his old-fashioned hat to the gusts tugging at it. With a quick grab he anchored it once more as he scurried off toward the bluff road. I wish I could have caught him. Why was I seeing him here?

"Success!" Charlie exploded out of the store's front door and leaped in front of me. "Let's go. The guy said this should do the trick. I just bet a gold coin is waiting inside that bottle for me."

"And now, while we're stuck inside because of the storm, you two can put notes in those bottles you found," Grauntie said as she walked up behind him.

"Remember, I want to go back up to the third floor again Grauntie," I said.

"That's okay. I'm planning on exploring more of the house myself. And of course, watching the storm come across the lake. It should be pretty dramatic. I imagine we'll be inside for a while, so we'll have time to do it all."

As soon as we made the turn toward the Pelletier house, I saw them. Henry stood next to a woman on the edge of the bluff. Her hand grasped the handrail of the steep set of stairs leading down to the beach. Her clothes billowed out around her...the winds whipping them senselessly one way then another. Her hair pulled and twisted in snarls around her head as she stood staring out at the water.

I saw no reaction from Grauntie or Charlie who walked right by. They couldn't see my imagining.

Not only were Henry's clothes old-fashioned, so were the woman's. A tightly fitted bodice hugged her figure above the wildly whipping skirt. She clutched a fringed shawl struggling to keep it over her shoulders as the wind tried to claim it.

The wind won. I watched the silky red shawl spin off her, swirling up and away. Stolen by the storm.

I raced to try to grab it. That's when she noticed me. And that's when I was close enough to see the tear streaks across her cheeks.

Henry saw me too now and grasped my hand. "You've come to us. I hoped you would. Please help

Clarisse. This might be the time. It feels right. I think they will come tonight. Tonight. The third floor. Promise me." His voice fading…

"Who will come?"

I heard Grauntie call my name and in the second it took for me to turn and give her an I'm-coming-wave, Henry and the woman were gone. I tried to imagine them back. I couldn't. It was frustrating. Would I ever be able to control my imaginings? Clarisse? Where had I heard that name? Then it came to me. Dorothy told Grauntie that Clarisse was the last Pelletier to live in the house. Was it her I'm supposed to help?

Grauntie waited, holding the door open for me as I ran the last way toward the house. I raced right past, grabbing the light bulb from her. In the kitchen, Charlie was already applying the oil to the lid. "It says to let it soak in for forty-five minutes."

I ignored him and ran up the stairs to the second floor, turned and raced to the top floor. The space was just as I'd found it. Dusty, closed up…holding only old memories. Or was there more here now? I put the new bulb in the lamp. I had to smile, it lit up okay last night…but I couldn't count on my imaginings to turn it off and on as needed! So, *a* new bulb and voila…light.

I saw the two huge portraits clearly now. The woman on the beach didn't look like the woman in the portrait.

Was this a painting of Clarisse? Or was Clarisse the little girl from last night? No, she was that woman with Henry on the bluff. My head is spinning.

Last night the little girl said they never came back. Who did she mean? Her mother and father? Who did Henry mean when he said they will come tonight? Tonight…I promised the little girl I will be back tonight. Soon I'll figure this out.

24

DISCOVERED

"Man, that was one of the stupidest, most pigheaded, selfish things you've ever done," the dive master screamed at Liam. "I can't believe you would put everyone in danger like that!"

"What more do you want me to say? I apologized. And we're all back safe and sound," Liam said.

Abby just shook her head. "You don't get it do you? All the rules regarding dive buddies and scuba diving safety said I should have left you down there when you refused to go up."

"And you might add I pushed you away," Liam said, hanging his head.

"I forgot about that!" Abby's jaw clenched. "I broke the group's rules and my own when I returned to find you. I risked my own life."

"Abby, I'm really sorry. And I'm eternally grateful you did. It was stupid. I know that."

The other divers, done with all the arguing and rehashing of what had happened, decided their hunger couldn't be ignored any longer. "Abby you coming with? Or want us to bring you something?"

Liam, looking crestfallen, said, "What about me? Even a jerk has to eat."

One of the group punched Liam's arm just a little too hard. "Ouch! Is that out of your system now?" Liam rubbed his arm. "And will you bring me something to eat?"

"Yeah, I will. But don't forget…we're all still mad at you."

Liam joined Abby where she was working on her computer downloading the newest photographs from Liam's camera.

"You deserved all of that," she said without looking up from her work.

"Hey, I'm sorry. Especially pulling you into that danger. I can't believe how quickly that storm got here," Liam said. "Is the download done?"

"Hang on, I'm doing some enhancing to make things as clear as possible."

"I know I saw a vessel. And these photos will confirm it! That was no glare, reflection, or shadow this time."

Abby kept her head down, peering at the screen and typing on the keyboard.

"I'm eternally grateful you rescued me," Liam said in a low voice.

Abby looked up, excitement in her eyes. "And I'm glad I did too."

Liam felt a lump rise in his throat as Abby slowly smiled at him.

"You are?" Liam said in a tentative voice, his heart racing. Was she hitting on him? He wasn't good at flirting, but he tried. "May I ask why?"

Abby laughed out loud. "Not that you goof...this!" She spun the laptop screen so Liam could see what was on it. "You've discovered a new wreck!"

"I knew it!"

The elderly owner of the dive shop walked in. "What's going on in here?"

Liam turned the laptop screen toward him. "We've found another wreck near the Sandusky."

"That's a big claim to make," Joe said.

Abby said, "He's right Joe. These photos confirm it. They only pick up a portion of it, but it's an important piece that might allow us to identify the ship."

Joe rested his knuckles on the desk and leaned in. "Let me take a look at that." He studied the photograph on the screen for a few moments.

Finally, Abby broke the silence. "Liam saw it. The water in the area seemed so stirred up around it. Like the currents were swirling and pushing against us. I didn't actually see it, but Liam managed to get these shots of it."

Joe stood, straightening up and rolling his old creaky shoulders, still not saying a word.

"I think that might be the ship's figurehead. I know it looks like it's just floating unattached, but if it wasn't for the deep cloudiness in the photograph, you'd see that it's part of a larger thing. The body of the wreck." Liam said, trying to convince Joe. "But then the storm came, and we had to turn around."

"You're darn right you had to turn around. The foolish actions of you two put everyone on that boat at risk," Joe said.

"Here let me try to enlarge it a little more," Abby said, choosing to ignore Joe's comment.

"Scared the bejesus out of me. Just poking up, coming out of nowhere. Looks like some sort of bird, maybe?" Liam could barely contain himself. He wanted Joe to see what he'd seen.

Joe, a man of few words, simply said, "I see it Liam. I might know a bit about it. Based on these images I'd guess it's from the turn of the century."

The next thing Liam knew the divers returned with hamburgers and fries.

"Find that mysterious phantom wreck yet Liam? The one you risked your life for?"

"Or was it the mysterious monster of the Mackinac floating by?"

"Oh, how about a sunken city where the fishies play?"

"Ohhhh…spooky!

"Hey Liam, this is a mystery story for you to write. The Phantom of the Lake."

"Or Mystery in the Deep! No wait…"

Liam held up his hands. "Ha ha. Very funny. Listen up. Joe here saw what I photographed, and he knows more about the ship." He turned to Joe. "So, tell us."

The group, now suddenly silent, gathered closer to hear what Joe had to say. Outside the wind howled around the small building on the shore of the dark and storm whipped lake.

Joe looked at the other divers. He had to tread carefully here. If his hunch was right, this was big. He didn't speak.

"How come no one ever found it if it was so close to this other wreck?" someone said. "Seems hard to believe."

Why wasn't Joe joining the conversation Liam thought. Come on man, help me out here.

"Tell you what, let me do some research." Joe looked up at the other divers gathered around. "And we'll go back down as soon as possible to check it out."

The unexpected announcement excited the group. For Joe to jump in like this it had to be something big.

Liam looked dismayed though. "Oh man, I've got to get back to work."

"Thought you were a writer, can't you make your own hours?" One of the group said.

Liam laughed. "Sort of. But right now, I still have a so-called real job to support myself."

"Maybe this find really will make a good mystery for you to write," Abby offered.

Liam nodded. "I'll have to think on that. But now I'm starved. Let's eat."

Joe turned to leave. "You guys lock up."

25

LILLIA

I found Charlie sitting at the kitchen table struggling to pull a deep blue velvety bag out of the old bottle.

"Wait, let me help." Grauntie took the bottle from him. "You need to twist the fabric a little. It should pull through the neck. You need to be careful. Don't tear it."

Despite being distracted thinking about who I would see upstairs tonight, I was excited for Charlie. How random was finding that bottle on the beach today? I sat down at the table with them, resting my chin on my crossed arms and watching their efforts to get the bag out of the bottle.

Grauntie finally worked the material into a twisted shape by spinning it around a pencil and got it out. She began to untie the delicate gold cording that gathered the top of the bag together.

"I get to see inside first," Charlie said, practically bouncing out of his chair.

"Don't worry…I'll let you," Grauntie told him.

"Calm down Charlie. It's not going anywhere," I said. He was getting a little wacko. A gold coin? Fat chance that is what's in the bag.

Grauntie paused in her efforts and held the bag in her palm. "This is a lovely bag." She spoke slowly, enunciating each word carefully. "I don't know if I've ever tried to unknot such a fragile feeling thread."

I had to laugh! She was torturing Charlie…dragging it out like that. He didn't get it though and just kept his eyes on the bag. His hands hovering over it.

I decided to play along. "Grauntie, I think you should rest a bit and leave that until morning. It's been a long day."

That got his attention. "Knock it off Lillia. Come on Grauntie! Are you playing with me?"

"Sorry. Here you go. Fingers crossed for a rare gold coin to be inside!"

Charlie spread the small velvet bag open.

26

LONG AGO

Over one hundred years ago…

Louisa Pelletier was nervous. She had been so for hours. Their yacht sailed safely through rough waters before, certainly this time would be no different. However, her unease persisted all afternoon and into the evening hours. She trusted the Cygnet's captain, he was one of the best. When he expressed his concern about the speed of the approaching storm Louisa took it seriously, but she was torn. Did my dear husband Maurice, knowing how badly I wanted to get to Mackinac Island, force the captain's decision to sail past the last safe harbor? Had my own impatience to reach my child, who waited on the island just beyond these treacherous Straits of Mackinac, put us all in danger?

Settled into the master cabin below deck for the remainder of their voyage, Louisa said a prayer that all would be well. The effect of the rough lakes waters on the Cygnet was obviously increasing. She had already put things away in the cabinets so they wouldn't start flying off of surfaces. She had prepared herself for arrival on Mackinac Island, whenever that would be. Choosing a lovely blue dress and her new diamond earrings, Louisa was now left to wait it out.

Louisa smiled. Secretly she was glad to get to her little girl before the storm did. Poor dear was afraid of many things…and storms was one of them. Now she could cuddle Clarisse so she wouldn't be afraid.

Her precious little swan. So beautiful, so gentle. Both her and Maurice were disappointed that Clarisse simply could not tolerate sailing. Dear child barely made it across to the island on the ferry. The Thatcher's had to try to catch her at nap time, so she wasn't aware she was on the water. Maybe one day Clarisse would grow out of the fear that overcame her. I hope she learns to love sailing as much as her father and I do.

To that end, Louisa had commissioned their jeweler to create an exquisite swan pendant for Clarisse. She'd carefully put it in a deep blue velvet bag and then tucked that inside a lovely blue glass bottle. She planned on planting it on the shoreline as though it had just washed ashore. When it was found by the child, she would read her the note...

Whoever finds this silver swan,
Need fear the seas no more.

Louisa held that blue bottle in her hands. She clutched it against her as she envisioned acting amazed...surprised by Clarisse finding the bottle and the note. I'll tell her that our family emblem is a swan. That our yacht's name is that of a young swan. That she must have found this because it is a special totem to protect her when she sails. It will become her good luck charm. She will wear it and be afraid no more.

On the top deck, Maurice was anxious as well. This storm had grown with startling speed. Its power evident by the suddenly strengthening winds. Had they been mistaken not to take shelter earlier? Now the rains drove against them horizontally. The winds whipping the sails. The sails must be taken down at once!

Above the howling, a sharp boom sounded. One of the masts! Maurice grabbed at a railing as the yacht began rolling under the loss of the sail. The crew scrambled in the pelting rain and violent winds to fight for control. They hurried to get the other sails down. Their only hope now was to stay afloat and let the storm take them where it would.

The Cygnet was not only exquisite in its beautiful design but also built to the most exacting standards of sea worthiness. She will survive this Maurice thought.

The captain approached him. "I fear the Cygnet may not be able to withstand the rolling and twisting much longer sir," he shouted to Maurice.

"Thank you, Captain," Maurice answered. With a forced calm he said, "Are the life rafts prepared for everyone?"

"Yes sir."

"Well then let's see how she does. I believe the winds are pushing toward the northern shore of Canada."

"Yes, that is my sense too. The closer we get to the shoreline before we abandon ship the better."

"Very well. I'll go below and tell my wife."

With rain pelting against him, Maurice struggled to get to the stairs to find Louisa. He didn't make it. The Cygnet spun sideways into a tall wave. The captain and the crew saw what was happening. Maurice and Louisa did not.

The Cygnet rolled and began sinking immediately.

No life rafts were launched.

No distress signals were given.

No one survived.

A small object floated to the surface. The blue bottle danced with a rolling and flipping rhythm on the waves. Playfully it popped up and down…bobbing away from the watery grave of the Cygnet.

At Joe's Dive Shop the late night gathering broke up shortly after Joe left. Liam knew he would need to head back to the island again tomorrow as he'd promised. The Pameroys were nice people. The storm was still in the area as he and Abby walked outside.

"Abby, when do you think you'll dive to the wreck again?"

Abby locked the door behind her before turning to him to say, "Not sure. We know there's something down there so I'm excited to get back to explore it. Right now, I've got to run. My dog's all alone and she hates storms. We'll be in touch with you about what you found. I think Joe knows more than he was willing to share tonight."

"Me too. I'll try to get back here tomorrow then. Do you think he knows what ship it is?"

"Could be. Night Liam."

He watched Abby's figure run through the wind and rain toward her car.

27

LILLIA

"It's only a necklace," Charlie said when he opened the little sack. He dropped it on the table, his disappointment showing in the way his whole body slumped.

"But look there's a note here too!" Grauntie said. "That's pretty neat. Right?"

I could see she was trying to distract Charlie, so I played along. "A note? Let's read it."

Whoever finds this silver swan,
Need fear the seas no more.

A small tingle went through me. What a quirky note, like something in a fortune cookie. You read it, and then tried to figure out how it applied to you. Hmm, Charlie found the bottle and the silver swan. But he didn't fear the sea, he loved it. I took the note and tucked it in my pocket.

Grauntie quickly moved on by asking Charlie, "I can see you're disappointed in this. Can you think of something better to put in your bottle?"

"A gold coin," Charlie said, still in a pout.

"Ha ha smartie. I mean something you could easily get. A photograph or brochure of the island? Do a *guess where I am* kind of thing for whoever finds the bottle? How does that sound?"

"I'll think about that. Maybe. I guess. I'm kind of tired now. See you in the morning Grauntie," Charlie said, giving her a kiss on the cheek before walking away.

"Jeez, was he serious? He was really expecting some Spanish gold coin? A slight possibility on the shore in Alabama where he hunted for treasure, but seriously? On Lake Huron?"

"Now Lillia, you were young once too. And young ones believe that almost anything is possible," Grauntie said. "In fact, if I started sharing some stories about your imaginings Charlie wouldn't believe them."

"Don't you dare. I have enough trouble with Mom."

I picked up the necklace. The swan pendant had beautiful detailing. You could see the etched feathers clearly even though the piece looked tiny, like it was meant for a child.

"How come this didn't get that funny looking, weird blackish color on it?"

Grauntie said, "It's probably not real silver. Just a cheap imitation that some kid put in the bottle."

"I don't think so. Here look at it." I handed the necklace to Grauntie.

She inspected markings on the clasp. "You're right. This is not a trinket. I suppose it's not showing tarnish, which is that blackish stuff you asked about, because it was stored in the bag and sealed in the bottle. Any sterling silver exposed to air will tarnish."

"I wonder how long it was in the water?" I picked up the bag. It was a soft fabric in a vivid blue color. I read what was embroidered in gold lettering on the side of the bag.

July 17, 1889
  Miller's Fine Jewelry
  Chicago, Illinois

I slipped the bag in my pocket too.

Grauntie, still admiring the piece, said, "The chain is

exquisite. Such fine links and woven in such an intricate manner. Why on earth anyone would put this in a bottle and send it out is beyond me."

"Can I keep it?"

"Fine by me. Your brother doesn't want it that's for sure."

"Could you help me close the clasp," I asked as I held the chain around my neck and turned my back to Grauntie.

The swan felt warm against my skin. I fingered it gently. Grauntie was right. Why would anyone just send it off in a bottle?

Strange.

28

STORMY NIGHT

The rain pounding against the windowpanes, the wind howling across the island. I wouldn't want to be out in this one Nora thought, grateful to be safe and dry inside. She'd made sure any open windows were closed. No sense letting any water damage occur. She poured herself a glass of wine, turned out the first-floor lights, and walked upstairs.

Lillia was coming out of the bedroom she shared with Charlie.

"Grauntie, I want to go up to the third floor and look around some more. Can you check on Charlie? I think he's nervous about the storm."

"Sure. Did you get that lightbulb put in so you can see what you're doing?"

"Yep. I put it in right when we got back."

Grauntie was glad Lillia was enjoying herself. She always found something to do when they traveled together. Lillia loved old houses and having that attic unlocked for her was a treat. *I wonder if something is going on with her imaginings again. Thank goodness I'm around to support her. My brother, her grandfather, had some specialness too. He tried to explain it to me, but I just didn't get it. And I still don't understand what Lillia can do, but I accept it. Sure wish her mother could appreciate her special abilities and not be afraid of them.*

Charlie was still awake when Grauntie Nora walked into his room.

"Hey big guy. Sorry about it just being a necklace in the bottle. Were you lying awake here thinking about what to put in your bottle to send out?"

"Sort of," he mumbled.

"Want to talk? Are you afraid of the storm?"

"It's not that. I'm a big boy," Charlie said indignantly.

"Oh, good then. I was going to sit out on your balcony and enjoy my wine. I want to watch the storm coming in over the lake. But if that would bother you and keep you awake, I won't do it."

He quickly answered. "You can sit out there. I don't mind."

She walked by his bed with a small smile on her face. "Oh good. Thanks."

"Let me know if you get scared out there. I'll be right here," Charlie said, yawning and turning on his side.

"I will." There, that should settle him.

She stepped out to the covered deck, grabbing the small quilt hanging over a chair to wrap around her shoulders. She moved one of the chairs tight against the wall, getting as far away from any rain blowing in.

She watched lightning bolts shoot down out of the dark night clouds. A deep booming rumble sounded above before slouching away with distant low grumbles. Between the sights and sounds, endless drumbeats of rain soothed Nora. Yes, she loved a good storm.

Now fully engulfed by the battering storm and at its mercy, the lake churned madly.

In the deep black darkness, lightning strikes illuminated the marking buoy for the Sandusky shipwreck. It was but a tiny spot atop the rough surface of the lake. It was being dragged by the wild waves pounding relentlessly against it. But no worries, for such markers would be repositioned when the storm was over. Markers to indicate shipping lanes, drastic changes in water depths, underwater obstacles, and of course, shipwrecks. Things would return to normal. The lake would settle. The sun would come out. The ships would leave their safe harbors.

Deep beneath the tempestuous wild turbulence on the surface, in the depths of the cold waters, the Sandusky shipwreck remained unmoved. Still. As it had been for decades.

Nearby, the Cygnet stirred and righted itself.

29

LILLIA

With Charlie gone to bed, and Grauntie sipping her wine and watching the storm move through, I made my way back up to the third floor. Finally, the night could begin!

Glad I'd put that light bulb in earlier. I switched it on and sat in one of the plump armchairs. I wiggled my butt around to find a comfy spot, ready to wait as long as necessary.

No telling how long I'd be here watching for Henry and Clarisse. Earlier, when I saw her and Henry standing on the bluff, I didn't do anything to make them appear. Mostly my imaginings just pop in like that. It would feel so much better if I could control them though. So instead of sitting here waiting, I could say, *Hey Clarisse, you can come out now. I'm here. Let me know what's up...* and she'd appear!

Grandpa had tried explaining my special ability a few times. How I can pull left behind energies together and see things in them. Something in me is like a magnet for the fragile pieces of energy life leaves behind. It was such a confusing explanation to a child. Then he finally just said…*Lillia, we don't understand electricity, but we use it. It's sort of like that. Trust yourself little one. It'll be fine.* And so, I've been working with my imaginings as best I can ever since.

The room was shot through with a burst of brightness as a lightning bolt hit nearby. Objects in the room revealed themselves…strange startling images in the bluish light…then, just as fast, gone! Images sent back to wait in the gloom outside the lamp's light.

I braced for the thunder coming. It engulfed the house, vibrating my bones with its deep bass rumbles. I grasped the swan pendant as I listened to the thunder fade away.

Calm down Lillia.

You need to clear your mind. I should try meditating. That's it! I took a deep breath and blew it out, resting my hands on my knees.

Breathe deep in.

Thoughts pushed out.

Breathe in.

Push out.

Whoa, I was getting lightheaded.

Still alone.

No Clarisse.

No Henry.

Okay one more time.

Close my eyes.

Breathe.

In.

Out.

"It was a storm far worse than this. They didn't stand a chance." A presence in the chair next to me spoke. "I spent the rest of my life hoping it wasn't true."

Dare I open my eyes? I did a squint peek. It was her. The woman standing on the bluff. I did it! Clarisse is here with me.

"So often I dreamed that they would just appear… sitting in these chairs one more time. I'd ask them where have you been? They would smile and say nowhere sweet daughter. We've always been right here with you. Then I'd go back to playing with my toys. Dreams can be cruel."

I watched her staring off towards the wall where the two large portraits leaned. So, this was the playroom of Clarisse Pelletier. Here's where she played with her toys waiting for her mother and father to arrive. Those people in the large portraits.

"The waking up was the worst. But I never gave up hope. Never."

I saw tears run down her wrinkled cheeks. Cheeks that not been kissed by her parents since she was a little child.

"Mother promised me she and father would arrive on the island soon after I did. But then the storm hit. I waited all that night. Then the next day and the next and the next." A sob escaped her lips.

She turned to me, extending her arms. "Look at me now. Her little girl grew old."

My heart ached for her. What a sad story.

"As time went by, I knew they would never come sailing into the harbor. In my head I knew that to be true. But my heart refused to accept that truth. I moved their portraits up here...and waited. And I grew old. My heart wore out with the waiting, the hoping. It failed me...quietly one night...alone. It just finally gave out and released me from this beautiful earthly waiting room."

Her lips started trembling but then stopped. Her eyes grew big and round as she stared at my throat. Slowly she reached her hand toward me. "What is that on your neck?"

30

DREAMS OF FLYING

Charlie rode a small boat up and down big waves. The boat, shaped like a swan with an elegantly arching neck, was like a ride at an amusement park. Then suddenly the boat became a real swan and dove into a wave…popping up on the other side…shaking the water off her head.

Then zoom, down into the depths of the lake…where thousands of blue bottles floated past.

Charlie clung to her neck with one hand…laughing, feeling the water rushing past him…while his other hand reached toward the bottles. But before he could claim one…back up to the surface they went.

Again! Again! Charlie shouted.

The swan spread her wings like giant sails and rose high up through the clouds. The lake, the land, the entire earth shrunk beneath them.

Charlie grew fearful. No! Go back! He looked down and earth appeared as a colorful marble below them. They flew higher as the swan ducked and dived between clouds. Clouds shaped like bottles…like carriages…like ships.

The air was thin…Charlie gasped for breath…

Heavy black clouds darkened the horizon. A storm was moving in.

Take me back…

* * *

While Charlie, tucked under the quilts in his bed dreamed, Grauntie watched the storm over the lake.

This had been another good trip with the kids. Too bad Charlie was disappointed in what he found in the blue bottle. Quite unique to discover such a lovely piece of jewelry. No more fearing the sea the note had said.

I wish there was a charm that erased Jennifer's fear of her daughter's imaginings. But at least Lillia didn't let her mother's feelings weigh on her so heavily anymore, which was good.

Grauntie took a sip of her wine as the lightening spilt the distant sky.

While Charlie dreamed and Grauntie sipped, Liam lay in his bed unable to sleep. He could taste success. He imagined doing interviews on television about the newly discovered shipwreck. He'd create a mystery story around it and would become famous.

The storm was moving off now, away from St. Ignace.

31

LILLIA

"This?" I reached for the swan necklace. Clarisse asked me if she could see it. Why, in the middle of her sad story, would she want to see my necklace? I took the pendant in my hand, holding it out and away from my neck so she could see it better in the cone of light.

"Where did you get it?" Clarisse said softly.

"My brother found it in a bottle washed ashore at the beach. Just down the stairs from where I saw you and Henry earlier."

She looked up at me with a quizzical expression. "You saw me there?"

I nodded. "You were with Henry Thatcher."

It seemed she was trying to remember something. "I'm not really sure. I've seen so many storms pass by, but this time it was something stronger that pulled me. I felt I had to go closer to watch it coming in."

Then I gasped as I felt the clasp at the back of my neck being opened. Whose hands had done that? Shivers went through me. I sat frozen to the spot. The clasp released, and I caught the necklace as it dropped from my neck. It hung in my palm, the chain draping down away from the beautifully etched silver swan.

Clarisse's eyes were locked on the silver swan, tears glistening on her cheeks. "I've seen this in countless dreams. Dreams of my mother. Dreams of my father. I don't know what it means. But there is a reason you found it and you found me."

She took a deep cleansing breath and looked out into the stormy night. "I always thought it was a symbol of the hope I carried. Dreams that the Cygnet would come. But now you have brought it to me. You have brought my dream to life."

"What do you mean?" I kept my eyes on Clarisse. "Why a swan? What is the Cygnet?"

Clarisse took the pendant from my open hand. She stood and walked toward the two large portraits. "Cygnet means young swan. It was the name of the yacht Mother and Father were sailing on when they disappeared. It was the summer of 1889 and we were going to spend the season here on the island."

She seemed in a trance as she spoke, staring at the portraits of her parents. "I'd gone ahead with my nanny and her husband, the Thatchers, because I was terrified of sailing. I even cried the whole time on the ferry from St. Ignace. It's been endless...my regrets of not being with them on the Cygnet."

Fear of the water? The note! I pulled it from my pocket and held it up. "This note was with the necklace."

Clarisse suddenly spun around. Her thin figure hurried back to me. "A note? Show me!"

I held the paper out to her. Her eyes quickly scanned the message.

"This is for me Lillia! The message and the swan have reached me. They are coming. This time they are coming!" She grabbed the note, kissing it over and over. "I know it! I just know it! This necklace has to mean that. That's why I went to the edge of the bluff. That's why you're sitting here."

"I don't know about..."

"Please wait with me. I don't want to be alone again tonight."

32

STRANGE FOG

Mackinac Island lost electrical power during the night. When morning arrived, an unusually dense fog engulfed the island. When the wind died down an unnatural calm lay across the land. Power generators kicked on automatically to keep the ice cream frozen and the fudge chilled. Island people had seen this happen many times and were prepared.

The Pelletier house did not have such a generator and Grauntie moved about in the dim morning light. She peeked in the kids' room. Charlie was still sleeping. But where on earth was Lillia? She wasn't in her bed.

Grauntie searched downstairs, on the porch. No Lillia. This wasn't good. She ran to look outside and discovered the dense fog wrapping itself around the house. No sign of Lillia. Where had she gone?

Then she remembered. Grauntie ran up the flight of stairs to the third floor and threw open the door. There she was! Lillia lay curled up into a ball, asleep in a big comfy chair. Grauntie breathed a sigh of relief. I'll let her sleep.

So, this was the attic that tempted Lillia. Quite nice really Nora thought. More of a getaway room. Two big chairs and a lamp to read by sat on a lovely Oriental rug. Old furniture pieces were pushed away under the eaves, typical attic stuff, but overall not an abandoned feeling here. It felt like someone used this every day.

Why I bet you could see forever from here…if the fog wasn't so crazy thick! She walked toward the door that led to a small outside deck. Spooky. Like I'm in a cloud above everything. I can barely see to the ground three floors down she thought. But then below her, on the front walk something seemed to be moving about. Who would be here at this hour?

"Good morning," Grauntie Nora shouted. "Up here. Third floor! Can I help you with something?"

The person's head tilted up. She couldn't make out what was said. Nora cupped her hands around her mouth and shouted back. "I'm sorry I can't hear you. I'll be right down."

33

LILLIA

I opened one eye, then quickly closed it again. It was morning. Someone was talking. I snuggled down in the chair trying to fall back asleep…but popped back up!

Oh no! I'd been waiting with Clarisse. Did I actually fall asleep during an imagining? That had never happened before. They didn't come for her. Or did they? Things started to come together in my sleepy mind. She'd told me about her parents sailing to the island. But for some reason they didn't arrive. She thought I was here to help them find her. Or her find them?

I slumped, hanging my head. Clarisse was gone! I didn't help her. I failed her. I fell asleep! How stupid is that? Big shot imagineer Lillia Pameroy. Henry is going to be impressed with what you did. Not!

And we leave today! I took a deep breath. Pull yourself together. You still have today to figure it all out.

It was Grauntie I'd heard talking. For some odd reason she was on the third-floor balcony. "Grauntie? What's going on?"

She stepped back into the attic. "Morning Lillia. You gave me a scare when you weren't in bed this morning. You must have had some fun time exploring up here last night."

I almost told her everything I'd seen but that wouldn't help me now. I simply asked, "Is the storm over?"

"Yes, it's blown through but left a very thick fog behind. Someone is on the sidewalk outside. I'm going down to see who it is. Oh, and by the way, no electricity. Power's probably out across the whole island."

I decided to follow her down. I was super excited when I saw that it was Henry outside. I can tell him what happened last night, and he'll know what's up. But I would have to wait to get him alone.

Henry had come to check on us he told Grauntie. I listened as the two of them discussed the storm and the strange fog. Finally, he said, "Lakeshore Diner will be open. They have a generator. I'll walk down with you if you want. The paths are slippery with the thick fog."

"That sounds great. Can you give me a few minutes to wake Charlie and get us ready?"

"Of course. I'll wait right here."

As soon as she was gone, I said, "Henry, I saw her last night. Clarisse talked me! She told me someone was coming to get her, and she was so happy. She asked me to wait with her, but I fell asleep. I'm so sorry Henry. I failed."

Henry patted me, trying to calm me down. "Whoa, slow down. You did fine. It'll be all right. Tell me what happened before you fell asleep."

"Her story was so sad. She told me about her family. How as a little girl she was so afraid of sailing that she'd be sent on the train to northern Michigan with the Thatchers. That's you right?"

Henry smiled. "Yep that's me in your story. When I learned you were coming, I knew you could help us. Now finish your story about last night."

"Well, she talked about being scared on the ferry ride to the island. How she'd close her eyes and cuddle tight against Mrs. Thatcher, terrified for the whole time crossing the Straits to get to Mackinac."

Henry said, "I remember those times. My wife was so good with little Clarisse. Sweet little thing."

"She wished she had been able to face her fears and take that trip with her family. Then they'd all be together. Instead she was left behind, all alone on the island. Why didn't they arrive Henry? Why did they leave their daughter?"

Henry brushed aside my question. "Is there anything else you can tell me?"

"No, I must have fallen asleep." My hand flew to my neck. "The necklace. It's gone!"

Henry grabbed my shoulders, an expectant look on his face. "A necklace? Did it have a silver swan pendant on it?"

"Yes it did! But how did you know?"

He hugged me before saying, "I knew because Clarisse's mother told me she'd be bringing it up on that trip. She wanted to have Clarisse discover it on the beach as a good luck charm, something to cling to when she was afraid. Where did you find the necklace? I always thought it went down to the bottom of the lake with the yacht."

"The bottom of the lake? Oh no, did their yacht sink in a storm?"

"Yes, but tell me, where did you find the necklace?"

"Charlie found it in a bottle washed up on the shoreline. He finally got the cover off last night."

"Show me the bottle. Please. Hurry."

We quickly went to the kitchen, but the bottle and its rusted cap were both gone. "Oh, I'm so sorry. I messed this one up too."

"Not at all young imagineer Lillia. Not at all. I think the Cygnet is finally arriving here. The bottle doesn't really matter. I'm sure the necklace was meant for Clarisse."

We heard Grauntie and Charlie coming downstairs. Henry raised his finger to his lips, just like he'd done in the stable imagining, letting me know this was between us. It made me feel special. Henry offered Grauntie his arm as we left the house. "Goodness but this fog is dense!" Grauntie said as she walked arm in arm with Henry.

I could barely contain myself. I couldn't decide if I would let her know that the man she walked with wasn't alive. Funny how sometimes spirits can manifest themselves to living people. Maybe I'd tell her later…she'd be excited and not afraid at all.

"You are a true gentleman to help an old lady like me."

"My pleasure ma'am."

34

MYSTERIOUS FOG

Liam was on the first ferry out of St. Ignace this morning, heading across the lake to Mackinac. He was worried about the Pameroys in that old house. The storm had been a bad one. Plus, he knew they planned on leaving today and he was eager to tell Charlie that the dive had been successful. He'd seen the wreck again!

The fog was thick...heavy...a mysterious cold blanket. It was more than a fog. He felt he could scoop it, creating a hole to see through. He had to chuckle to himself. Was that the mystery writer in him coming out? The fog would lift eventually, just as it always did.

The ferry was not far out of the dock area when the engines throttled back. There was no obvious reason for them to stop. It was as if the entire ferry, and everyone on board was alone now, isolated on the lake.

A voice came out of the air. "Ladies and gentlemen."

Liam chuckled and looked around. It was only him and two other men aboard. No ladies riding to Mackinac Island. *Who am I to quibble?*

The voice continued. "We are unable to navigate safely through this fog bank. We will try to maintain our current position until it lifts, and we feel safe to continue on to Mackinac. We anticipate being able to get back underway shortly. Please sit back and relax. Thank you."

Liam was seated in the open-air portion of the ferry. He put his feet up on the empty seat across from him, intending to take a quick nap. He didn't get much sleep last night as thoughts of what he saw on the dive filled his mind.

In the unseen distance the longest, loneliest foghorn sounded. Foghorns always had a deep melancholy tone, Liam thought, but this one was new. The sound seemed to become part of him. It reverberated through his muscles.

Liam felt something pass close by. He sat back up, turning to look in all directions. There was no engine noise. No wind was blowing, but strangely he heard sails flapping. Sails couldn't be making a sound because this type of stillness was called a dead calm zone.

* * *

Sherry watched as the fog rolled in. Wait, it wasn't really rolling. It was dense, a curtain pulled over the diner's window. She'd never seen anything like it.

Thank goodness the generator kicked on last night when the power went out she thought, filling one of the coffee pots with water and coffee grounds. She was surprised people weren't here. No cook. No customers. Usually island people want to check out what's going on after a storm.

Sherry thought on that a moment more. Something's wrong. She peered out the front window again. The streets were eerily quiet. Empty.

She stepped outside the door and into the odd fog. She wrapped her arms around herself as a shiver ran through her. I can actually feel the air. Like I'm pushing through something alive. This wasn't the normal wet feeling fog. Her instincts told her to go behind the diner building to catch a glimpse of the dock. People would be opening the pier up. The ferries will be arriving shortly.

Walking between buildings and down slippery wooden steps put her out on the walkway that sat on a low wall running along the edge of the shoreline. She leaned against the rounded railing that protected walkers from slipping and falling down to the water below. Squinting, she made out the eerie outlines of warehouses and shipping offices lining the pier. Nothing's moving out there she thought just as the longest, loneliest foghorn sounded nearby.

She gasped. A large vessel slipped through the waters near her. Wait! She had seen something. Right? And it was still moving toward the dock. Wasn't it? What a strange sensation. She was afraid and slightly thrilled by what she might be witnessing. One of the spirit ships coming into the harbor?

Finally…she thought. After all these years of hearing about this, I'm feeling it. The vessel was a presence more than an actual object.

A shouted *ahoy* and the crisp snap of a sail startled her. She jumped back, slipping and falling, grabbing at the railing. As soon as she righted herself, she hurried back up the steps and between the buildings. She didn't stop moving until she was inside the diner again. Panting, trying to catch her breath, she braced her back against the door.

Her breathing slowed. With a deep swallow she stood straight up. Get a hold of yourself girl. You're a big talker about ghosts and spirits. It gets a little too close and bam, you're out of there. Scaredy cat! A knocking at the door caused Sherry to jump again.

Grauntie Nora opened the door a crack and peeked in. "Sorry, didn't mean to startle you. Are you open?"

Sherry stepped aside stuttering, "Oh sorry…just had

a bit of a scare. Ah, I was catching my breath. Come… come on in."

"What is going on? You looked like you saw a ghost," Nora said. "Henry here was kind enough to walk down here with us. It was a bit slippery with all the moisture in the air."

Sherry peered up and down the sidewalk. "Henry who?"

"Um, he had to take off Grauntie," Lillia said quickly. "Let's get inside. I'm starving."

"Me too," Charlie added.

"Hmm…okay," Grauntie Nora said, the puzzled look remaining on her face as she leaned back to look down the sidewalk searching for Henry too. What on earth? He couldn't just disappear.

35

LILLIA

Why had he disappeared? He hadn't talked anymore about Clarisse, so I still didn't know what was up. But I was glad Grauntie didn't ask any more about Henry being gone. I could tell it confused her. It would confuse anyone who had someone standing next to them one moment and then they literally disappeared the next.

After getting us seated, taking our orders, and pouring coffee for Grauntie, Sherry said, "You asked me if I saw a ghost. Well let me tell you..." She leaned in closer even though we were her only customers. "I think I saw a spirit ship just before you got here."

She straightened back up, an expectant look on her face. I don't know what she thought...maybe we'd laugh at her? We didn't get a chance to respond because the cook came hurrying in and Sherry excused herself.

Charlie mumbled. "What's a spirit ship?"

"I have no idea," Grauntie said. "But Liam's grandfather called this mystery island, so I suppose that's one of the mysteries."

Sherry came back to say since the cook had finally arrived our food would be out shortly.

"Charlie, ask Sherry your question," Grauntie Nora said.

Charlie seemed suddenly shy, so I spoke up. "We were wondering what a spirit ship is?"

Sherry was eager to share her story. "This island's harbor is particularly good for ships to shelter in when storms blow through. Legend has it that not only do real ones come, but so do the spirits of ships that have tried to travel through these treacherous straits and lost their way." Her voice took on a quavering tone, these last words drawn out slowly. "Ships the lake takes and never gives back. Ghost ships."

Charlie's mouth hung open and his eyes bugged out. I kicked him under the table. He blinked and let out his breath.

"Seriously?" Grauntie said. "Or are you kidding us? Teasing the tourists?"

Sherry said, "Cross my heart and hope to die, stick a needle in my eye if I'm not telling the truth. They slide in quiet like. Unseen by but a few. And today I was lucky enough to see one."

She was really getting into the story she was telling. I almost expected strange organ music to start playing.

"I walked around back earlier. It was so strange. Eerie like. Nobody but me here. Someone has to be on the dock by now I thought. When I leaned out over the railing to see, I was almost hit by the side of a big old sailing ship that floated on by." She stared at each of us in turn. "And a voice said *ahoy*. I never heard of anyone else ever hearing a voice from a spirit ship."

As I listened to Sherry's story, my eye was drawn to a carriage riding by. I couldn't believe it. There proud as could be, all dressed up with a stylish hat holding a white feather, rode Clarisse. Her hands rested on a small leather bag in her lap. Henry sat proudly erect on the driver seat, once again driving Clarisse Pelletier through the streets of Mackinac Island. I smiled.

Sherry was still talking. "As for me, now I know the spirit ships are real…in a paranormal way!" Sherry gave a sharp nod as though to erase any doubt.

I wanted to tell her that believed her. To let her know she is not alone in believing in ghosts and spirits. I have to think that the ship Sherry experienced passing by her in the thick fog was on its way to pick up a passenger. The Cygnet had come to Mackinac Island one more time for Clarisse Pelletier. She was going to board the family yacht. No doubt wearing her silver swan pendant, she would no longer fear the seas.

A broad smile broke across my face. Liam is walking in! Hooray!

36

PHOTOGRAPHS

The fog that had shrouded Mackinac Island for the past few hours was lifting. In the cozy atmosphere of the Lakeshore Diner, Sherry retold her story of the spirit ship. Customers listened politely. Some chose to agree with Sherry that the legend was true. Others silently dismissed the tale. But everyone was feeling better because the sun was breaking through and burning that awful fog off. The place was bustling again, just as it should be after a storm.

Meanwhile at the Pameroy table, Liam was sharing his story of the trip. How the ferry stopped to wait for the fog to lift and he had the sense of a ship passing in near him.

He overheard Sherry telling her story to a group of customers on a nearby table, but before he could compare stories with her, Charlie asked, "What about that ship-wreck? Did you find it again? Get better photos of it this time?"

"I did Charlie. Pretty good ones. My dive buddy Abby will enhance them on her computer to see if we can figure out what vessel it was. Abby and Joe, the dive shop owner, are researching it today. In fact, they're taking another dive, probably in a couple of days when the waters have a chance to calm down from the storm's action."

"Sounds exciting," Grauntie said. "But right now, it looks like the stores are open. Let's do a little souvenir shopping before we go back to pack up."

"We're leaving today? But I haven't put my message in a bottle yet."

"You have time Charlie. Don't worry. I'm planning on taking a midday ferry back to the mainland. Are you staying here Liam?"

"Nope, in fact I'll ride back with you. And if you have time, the dive shop is near the ferry dock where we'll be landing in St. Ignace. Maybe you'd like to check it out Charlie?" Liam said.

"Would I? For sure!" Charlie said.

The group left the diner and spent the next hour strolling the main street running through town. Everyone chose a t-shirt and a flavor of fudge to take home. Lillia picked out a homemade treat for her dog Tucker, plus a book about hauntings and mysteries on Mackinac Island.

"One day a book authored by Liam Schmidt will be sitting on these shelves," Grauntie Nora said.

"I sure hope so," Liam replied.

"Try to find something to put in your bottle Charlie. Maybe this key chain with the Round Island lighthouse on it? Or you could roll up a postcard and tuck it in?"

Liam was the one who finally found what Charlie considered the perfect thing, a photo booth where all of them piled in to make funny faces for the camera. Everyone wanted a set. The booth got good business from the Pameroys that day!

37

LILLIA

I felt happy on the walk back to the Pelletier house. This was all fitting together now. From Henry being the first person we met here on the island…to all the swan connections…to Charlie finding the bottle with the swan necklace inside. Clarisse reunited with her parents. The day's weather was turning out to be perfect. Balmy with just the gentlest breeze blowing in off the lake.

Turns out Charlie had the blue bottle. He decided he wanted to reuse it for his note in a bottle launch. He carefully wrote our names on the back of one of the photo booth strips. Of course he picked the one where we were all making the stupidest faces!

I too wrote a note to put in one of the green bottles we'd gotten from the stable. I wrote it to Clarisse wishing her safe travels and signed it *Love from imagineer Lillia Pameroy,* because that's what I am.

Charlie and I ran down the wooden steps to the rocky beach to throw our bottles in. Charlie asked me if I thought it was right for him to reuse someone else's bottle.

"I think it is perfect Charlie. What arrived in that bottle was meant to land here. It will travel the seas again, ending up right where it is supposed to. Wherever that may be!"

38

GHOST CARRIAGE

When all the bags were brought out, Liam locked up the house.

"I was hoping Henry might drive us again like he did when we arrived," Grauntie said. "I wanted to say goodbye to him."

"Who's Henry?" Liam asked.

"A lovely elderly man who was waiting to give us a ride when we landed. I figured your grandmother sent him."

Liam shrugged. "I don't know anything about that."

"It was the most beautiful carriage. Creamy leather seats. Polished wooden fenders curving over spoked wheels."

"That sounds like the one in the stables," Liam said. "Come on I'll show you."

Everyone made their way through the high weeds and grasses to the back of the property. Charlie ran around and opened the stable door he and Lillia found a couple of days ago.

"Did the one he used look like this?" Liam pointed to the dusty, spider web covered carriage leaning on its hitching arms, and swiped the dust away from the emblem on the side of it. "Best my grandparents could figure out, this was the Pelletier family crest."

"Looks like a swan," Grauntie Nora said. "I can't say I remember that. I was too busy looking around. But the seats and the big rear wheels…they sure look the same."

Charlie said, "I remember that thing on the side of it!"

"The crest?" Liam asked.

"Yeah. It was right at my eye level."

"I remember it too," Lillia added in a soft voice.

Grauntie looked at Lillia with pinched eyes. "Really. Odd. I didn't notice the swan crest. Well this is obviously not the carriage Henry was driving." She gave Lillia a quizzical look. "Let's head down to the harbor."

39

LILLIA

I breathed a sigh of relief. It was the carriage and I know Grauntie suspected the truth. She gave the *we'll talk later look* again. That talk came now because Liam and Charlie were quickly engrossed in yet another conversation about scuba diving and shipwrecks.

Grauntie held my arm enough to keep me back so we could talk. "What's going on here Lillia? This morning I find you asleep in a chair in the attic. Then this carriage thing. That was it wasn't it? The same carriage that picked us up?"

I nodded. I gave her a kiss on the cheek. "Things started happening pretty much as soon as we got here. Remember those sunglasses you thought you left in the carriage? I found them when Charlie and I were exploring out here."

"Wait, you found them where?"

"In that dusty old carriage in the stable Grauntie. I slipped them into the house and pretended that they were there the whole time."

Grauntie laughed. "Well now aren't you the clever one! But why go through that. Why not just tell me?"

"I didn't know what was going on. And I was with Charlie. I didn't want him to know something was happening. You know he'll just blurt it out to Mom, and I'll be back at square one with her."

"I was thinking about her last night. Do you think she'll ever accept your special abilities?" Grauntie put her arm around me. "I don't encourage you to hide things from your mom, but she is still having a hard time getting over losing Charlie's twin Chloe before she could be born."

I let out a huge sigh. "But give me a break! That was eight years ago. I was only four years old."

"I know," Grauntie said. "And you know it's not your fault. Right?"

"Yes Grauntie. Thanks to you, I do know it wasn't my fault. It's just easier to keep things like this away from Mom. Charlie being born alive had nothing to do with me. Neither did his twin Chloe not making it have anything to do with me. I'm beginning to understand that my *seeing* Chloe as a doll inside of Mom's tummy was the misunderstanding of a little four-year-old girl who didn't know what she was seeing or imagining."

Grauntie gave me a thumbs up. "Back to the attic. What happened there last night?"

"Oh look! That French couple is getting on the ferry with us! And yes, I'll tell you the rest of it later," I said, giving her a quick hug.

As the ferry left Mackinac Island, Grauntie settled in to chat with the Canadian couple about their travels. I overheard them telling her plans for the rest of their journey down the Mississippi. When they mentioned they were taking a riverboat cruise Grauntie's eyes lit up. "You'll stop in Hannibal, Missouri? I've always wanted to see that town. Ever since I read the *Adventures of Tom Sawyer.*"

Hmm…I felt another trip coming up for me!

Charlie was busy talking with Liam. I could hear the excitement in Liam's voice. Charlie was enthralled with the idea of being able to scuba dive and made bold predictions that he'd learn soon.

I watched the Pelletier house up on the bluff as we glided by on the lake. To anyone's eyes it was just another one of the summer cottages. I knew that the lonely figure no longer haunted it. Clarisse Pelletier was off sailing bright seas.

It had been a good trip. Now I was ready to head home. Home to my bedroom. Home to my dog Tucker.

40

THE CYGNET

The dive shop in St. Ignace was quiet today. No dive boats were being sent out. A couple of people were looking at diving gear and booking future trips.

Liam took a few minutes to show Charlie the gear scuba divers used, explaining that diving in these lakes required dry suits.

"I thought they were called wet suits," Charlie said. "Now you called them a dry suit. I don't get it."

Liam laughed. "We need the thermal insulating qualities these offer because the lake water is so cold. Especially at the depths we go to."

"How far down is the wreck you're going back to?"

"It's about eighty feet down. Like an eight-story building. Some are much deeper. There's a lot of training involved to safely dive to the depths of our local wrecks."

Joe had just entered the shop and overheard Liam explaining safety for divers. "Did you tell the lad about the dangerous thing you did day before yesterday?"

Liam ducked his head as Joe's question hung in the air between them. Grauntie and Lillia looked at Liam, waiting for him to respond.

With an embarrassed look, Liam said, "Ah…"

Joe slapped Liam on the back. "Even the best divers, including this young man, can make mistakes. I'll let him tell you about it. Right now, though I hope you'll join me in the back office. Abby is there already. I'd like to share what I discovered in my research."

As everyone crowded around the computer screen, Abby pulled up the enhanced image Liam's camera had captured.

"This must have been a beauty. The detail of that figurehead was created uniquely for this vessel and shows amazing craftsmanship," Joe said. "To those of us who research and study shipwrecks, this top of its class personal yacht going down without a trace was highly unusual. It created quite a stir in 1889. Subsequently a mystery has built up around it. No bodies or debris were ever found. The wreck was never located."

"You know what this wreck is?" Liam asked. "Tell us! I'm so excited."

"Slow down. Until we go back down to see the entire vessel, whatever I say here is speculative."

Grauntie was intrigued by what she was hearing and seeing. "You sound somewhat sure of what you're seeing though. May I ask how you came to the conclusion that this yacht went missing in 1889?"

"Of course, my dear lady. It's that." Joe's finger stabbed at the image on Abby's screen. "That figurehead is unique to one vessel. The Cygnet."

"What's a Cygnet?" Abby asked.

41

LILLIA

I couldn't believe what I was hearing. What I was looking at on a computer screen in St. Ignace. Is that part of the yacht the Cygnet?

Without thinking I spoke aloud. "It's a French word meaning young swan." All eyes turned to me. "The young swan or Cygnet is part of the Pelletier family crest. In France, the family adopted the swan as their family emblem. Their estate was famous for the beautiful swans who graced the grounds."

"That's right," Joe said, a tone of awe in his voice.

"We saw the swan on their carriage!" Charlie shouted. "Right Lillia?"

"I don't know if you noticed, but I saw it was used on the china and silverware there too," Grauntie added.

Liam, swept up in the moment said, "And I've seen it on stationary in the desk at Grandma's house."

Joe raised his hands. "Now hold on everyone. How do you all know this? What does the Cygnet yacht have to do with a carriage and dishes and papers? And how, young lady, do you know about this Pelletier yacht?"

All eyes were on me again.

What had I done? How can I get out of this? I don't want to say a dead woman told me. How did I know about the family's estate? I must have forgotten much of what happened last night. I couldn't speak. Luckily Liam jumped in.

"My grandparent's summer cottage on Mackinac Island was originally built and owned by the Pelletiers. Can you believe it! Wow! We're the only other people who lived in it. Tons of old stuff was left when the last Pelletier died."

"Lucky you. Pretty fancy digs to get to live in!" Abby said. "And that's amazing that you have this connection to the shipwreck we're looking at. How did you know that though Lillia?"

Liam stopped a moment, before turning to me. "Abby's right. How'd you know all that? Oh, I remember now. You must have been exploring the attic. Did you see a photograph of the yacht there?"

Abby asked, "And how did you know that Cygnet meant swan? That's a pretty obscure word."

"Ah, um…" Oh gosh now what?

Charlie came to my rescue this time. He talked right over my hesitating mumblings. "Hey, I dreamed about a swan! I was flying on a swan's back. And then she dove under the water. It was a crazy fun dream! Until she took me too high…away up into the sky."

Grauntie slipped me a barely visible thumbs up, winked, and said, "Lillia just loves learning new things. I bet you probably looked it up in those old encyclopedias sitting on the bookcase at the house. Right?"

"Those wouldn't have that information," Liam said. "But seriously, however you knew it, that's pretty cool Lillia! So Joe, since the figurehead is a swan, is that how you knew where to start researching the yacht wreck I found?"

42

JOE'S STORY

Abby said, "I guess I can see how that might be a swan's head. And it sort of looks like wings in the carving behind it."

Joe said, "No maybe. No guess. That figurehead is a swan. That I am sure of. I've never seen it on photos of any other ship. Until we go down, I can't promise anything. But lord almighty, I don't know what else it would be."

Liam was amazed. "I can't wait to tell Grandma and Grandpa. What else do you know about it Joe?"

"The yacht was built for a wealthy Chicago family, the Pelletiers as Lillia mentioned. She was right, they were French, and their family had always used the swan as their symbol. Kind of ironic. Swans symbolize grace and beauty, music and poetry. Quite a departure from the fur trade that gave the family their wealth."

"How come no one else ever found the wreck?" Charlie asked.

"Good question. The lake is alive. Many downed vessels have not been found." Joe said.

Abby was amazed by it all. "Joe, do you know more about where it was heading or who was aboard?" "The Pelletiers were sailing to Mackinac Island for the summer. Should have found a harbor to shelter in. Instead the captain must have chosen to push on. Yacht disappeared off the face of the earth."

"This is really odd," Liam said. "What a great big small world it is. That I should discover the wreck of a yacht owned by the family of the house I spent my summers in."

"The guys were right last night. You'll have to write a mystery novel about it," Abby said.

"Thanks to Lillia, I'm going to explore the attic next time I'm there. Maybe I'll even set up a writer's loft in it. I'll open myself up to inspiration and look out across the lake and imagine what it was like all those years ago," Liam said.

Abby laughed. "I thought you had to get back to your real job!"

"Right, first that."

Joe nodded. "I rarely dive anymore, but I'll be leading a group down soon to verify that we've found the Cygnet. I'm excited. This will be quite an event in our world."

43

LILLIA

Grauntie and Charlie were still talking with Joe, Abby, and Liam as I slipped away. I needed fresh air.

Standing at the edge of Lake Huron I took in the beauty in front of me. A rainbow stretched up above the water. The serendipity of the Cygnet being found by Liam is such a twist. I love it!

When we left the island, and I knew Clarisse had reunited with her family, I figured that was the end of it. Now here I am leaving Michigan, knowing that there's so much more to the story. I was just looking at a photograph of part of the actual ship that sunk into the lake over one hundred years ago. And yet, it had just sailed out of Mackinac Island Harbor only hours ago...in a different form, but back on the water again. This is crazy amazing!

And how did that swan necklace in the bottle make it to our shore? Has it been floating in the lake ever since the yacht sank? Grandpa always said, there are things that humans, with our many limitations, can't explain.

* * *

It was three weeks later when we got a letter from Liam. It contained photographs and a copy of a newspaper interview he did.

The photos were of the Cygnet where it lay at the bottom of the lake. It was beautiful. Looking like it had simply and quietly sunk below the surface to get out of the storm…to rest awhile. Chairs still stood near a table. The engraved ship's bell hung in place. Dishes rested in their slots. Stained glass windows unbroken.

In his interview, Liam was quoted as saying that he was honored to have discovered the shipwreck. He told of finding old Chicago newspaper articles from the time of the storm. In one of them, friends told stories of the Pelletiers. They spoke of Maurice's pride in his extraordinary sailing vessel. Another family acquaintance, a well-known jeweler, told the sad story of a silver swan pendant necklace he had designed for the Pelletier's young daughter. He was saddened to think that now it lay on the bottom of the lake.

I reread that sentence twice. I had to. It validated what happened. It was all real. I was glad I'd kept the blue velvet bag the necklace came in. Clarisse ended up with the silver swan and I kept my own little souvenir. I doubt anyone will miss it.

In the interview, Liam went on to talk about his decision to take time off to write. He described making the third floor of the Pelletier house a writer's studio. The reporter ended by saying everyone would be looking forward to Liam's next book.

I would too.

ABOUT THE AUTHOR

A MESSAGE FROM THE AUTHOR

I really hope you enjoyed *Mystery Island*. It's the ninth book in my *Pameroy Mystery Series*. Each one will be set in a different state! I've got a lot of writing ahead of me... but I love it!

If you liked *Mystery Island*, I'd be very grateful if you'd leave a quick review on Amazon, Goodreads, or wherever you purchased the book.

You can visit my website for news and information. Be sure to check out photographs used as inspiration for in each book in the series. And you can sign up for my newsletter to learn when the next mystery will be published.

Happy reading... Brenda Felber

Web and email

facebook.com/brendafelberauthor

instagram.com/brendafelber

pinterest.com/bbfelber

goodreads.com/brendafelber

amazon.com/author/brendafelber

PAMEROY MYSTERY SERIES

Made in the USA
Monee, IL
29 December 2020